# Suddenly, Briony was afraid

Something was happening—had happened—
between them. And whatever it was, it had to be
stopped. She'd fled to Paris to clarify her emotional
state, not to complicate it.

"It is a beginning, isn't it?" the stranger persisted
gently, smiling at her in his will-sapping way.

"No!" She sounded unnecessarily harsh, but she
was panicking. A wild, forbidden excitement was
beginning to pulse through her, threatening to get
out of hand. Fear she could run from, but this other
feeling made her a willing captive.

"Yes," he contradicted bluntly.

"You don't understand," Briony told him hurriedly.
"I'm engaged. I'm going to be married. As soon as I
get back to England . . . I think."

**Anne Beaumont** started out as a Jill-of-all-writing-trades, but she says it was her experience as a magazine fiction editor, buying stories and condensing them for serialization, that taught her to separate the bones of a story from the flesh. In her own writing, she starts with her characters—"a heroine I can identify with, then a hero who seems right for her." She says that many writers work in reverse—plot first, then characters. "That's fine," she says. "If we all had the same method, we might all be writing the same books, and what a crashing bore that would be!" In addition to Anne Beaumont's romance novels, the author has written historicals under the pen name Rosina Pyatt. She lives on the Isle of Wight, with its sparkling white beaches, and has three children, of whom she is immensely proud.

## Books by Anne Beaumont

**HARLEQUIN ROMANCE**
3049—ANOTHER TIME, ANOTHER LOVE

**HARLEQUIN PRESENTS**
1231—THAT SPECIAL TOUCH
1391—SECRET WHISPERS

# A CINDERELLA AFFAIR
## Anne Beaumont

## *Harlequin Books*

TORONTO • NEW YORK • LONDON
AMSTERDAM • PARIS • SYDNEY • HAMBURG
STOCKHOLM • ATHENS • TOKYO • MILAN
MADRID • WARSAW • BUDAPEST • AUCKLAND

Original hardcover edition published in 1991
by Mills & Boon Limited

ISBN 0-373-03199-8

Harlequin Romance first edition June 1992

A CINDERELLA AFFAIR

# CHAPTER ONE

HEAD down against the driving rain and deep in
thought, Briony didn't hear a car door shut or see a
man sprint across the wide pavement of the boulevard in front of her. She just felt the shock of
impact as she walked straight into him. It was like
barging into a brick wall.

The breath whooshed out of her and she staggered
back. She raised her head instinctively and flinched
as the rain lashed her face like needles. She got a
brief impression of a tall and leanly powerful man,
then her heels slipped on the wet paving and she
began to fall.

The man reacted swiftly, his strong hands catching
her shoulders and steadying her. His grip was firm
and strangely comforting. For a crazy second she felt
protected, no longer alone and miserable in a
strange city.

Briony stood quite still in his clasp. Some deep
yearning within her craved to prolong these
moments of physical contact. Then her innate shyness overcame her, swamping her natural instincts
and flooding her with embarrassment. Oh, lord,
what if he sensed this strange effect he was having
on her?

Dazedly she took in how lithely handsome he was.
Tough, manly features, clear grey eyes fringed with
black lashes, a shock of unruly brown hair beginning

5

to darken and wave damply in the rain. Somewhere around thirty, she thought. He had the indefinable air of a man who had lived life to the full, and was impatient to do a whole lot more.

He was. . .he was the stuff that dreams were made of. Not her dreams, of course, because Matthew was so very different. And yet. . .

Briony's wayward thoughts cut out abruptly. She realised that by standing so passively and staring at him so openly, she might make this stranger think she was trying to pick him up. He was the type girls threw themselves at, if not quite as literally as she had.

Warm colour tinged her pale cheeks. She had no idea how adorably confused she looked, nor did she recognise the interest stirring in his eyes.

Her confusion increased as he began to speak. His French was much too fast for her to pick out any of the simple textbook phrases she knew. Floundering, Briony could only think vaguely how pleasantly deep his voice was. She could listen to him all day, even in the pouring rain. She began to wonder if their collision had knocked her silly. She wasn't normally like this.

He must have been more conscious of the rain than she was, for he released her shoulders, took her arm and led her under the awning of an elegantly façaded restaurant. It dawned on her that this must have been his destination when he had dashed across the pavement.

He was still speaking, and from his tone she knew he was apologising. Soon it would be her turn. She was frantically trying to string a few suitable words together when he fell silent and smiled at her.

It was a very attractive smile. Briony watched it start in his eyes, soften his tough features, crease his cheeks and lift the corners of his lips. Idiotically, she found herself yearning to reach out and touch those firm lips.

She couldn't understand what was happening to her. She could only blink at him, soft brown eyes bewildered, tremulous lips parted to utter words that wouldn't come. Finally she faltered, '*Pardon, monsieur. Je suis*. . .sorry, I mean, *je regrette*——'

'You're English,' he broke in, switching languages effortlessly. 'I should have known! That explains why you're so quiet—any self-respecting French girl would be blasting me for being so clumsy. Have I hurt you very much?'

'No, oh, no,' Briony denied, relieved she could stop trying to dredge up her schoolgirl French. It was true she felt bruised, but not in a physical way. It was more of an emotional disorientation, and its effect was lasting longer than the shock of physical impact. 'It was my fault, in any case. The rain was so fierce I wasn't looking where I was going.'

'Neither was I.' He spoke almost absently, his whole attention absorbed in looking at her.

It was flattering, but unnerving too. Briony became self-consciously aware she wasn't looking her best. She was dressed practically for an anonymous round of sightseeing, not an encounter of this kind. Men had been the last thing on her mind. Except for Matthew, of course.

Her dark stretch jeans, knee-length boots and red sweater had seemed good enough at the time. It hadn't been raining when she'd left her hotel, so she'd only carried her red raincoat as an after-thought. Now it was firmly belted around her, and she was afraid it made her look all the more dowdy.

Well, perhaps not dowdy, but not exactly alluring either. She wished she'd taken more care. She hadn't even bothered to make up properly, just a touch of lipstick that was probably worn away by now. That made her feel despondent enough, but mixed in with it was a twinge of guilt that she should be wishing to be more exciting.

She had no idea that her slender figure, bundled into a raincoat though it was, had its own waif-like charm. Nor did she suspect her rain-washed face had its own refreshing naturalness. Her complexion might be pale, but it was flawless, and her wide eyes were set at the same slightly upward slant as her cheekbones. Her lips were soft and full and inno-cently sensual. It was a pity that her thick black hair was drawn back into a French pleat and hidden under her hood, but a few strands plastered by the rain to her forehead and temples added a dramatic touch to her pale face.

Briony, wishing she looked entirely different, thought she was a mess, then her heart began to beat a little erratically as the stranger's eyes told her differently. She could read the interest in them now, it was so blatant. He was still staring at her with that concentrated intentness, and he didn't seem a bit bothered by the silence lengthening between them.

He didn't even seem to notice it, but Briony, lacking his assurance, was prompted by embarrass-ment to burble, 'Well, no harm's been done, and all's well that ends well, as they say.'

'What's ending?' he asked calmly. 'I thought something was beginning.'

Briony was taken aback. After less than twenty-four hours in Paris she'd already learned that Frenchmen flirted as lightly and naturally as they breathed. This stranger didn't sound as if he was flirting, though, more as if he was stating a fact.

With the jolt of an electric shock, she realised why. Something was happening—*had* happened!—between them. Suddenly she was afraid. Whatever it was, it wasn't right. It had to be stopped. She'd fled to Paris to clarify her emotional state, not to complicate it.

'It is a beginning, isn't it?' the stranger persisted gently, smiling at her in his will-sapping way.

'No!' She sounded unnecessarily violent, but she was panicking. A wild, forbidden excitement was beginning to pulse through her, threatening to get out of hand. Fear she could run from, but this other feeling made her a willing captive. What on earth was happening to her?

'Yes,' he contradicted bluntly.

'You don't understand,' Briony told him hurriedly. 'I'm engaged. I'm going to be married. As soon as I get back to England. . . I think.'

'You don't sound too sure about that.'

'Well, I am. At least, I will be as soon as—as I've sorted myself out,' she stuttered, sounding idiotic to her own ears.

His eyebrows drew together and he looked at her long and hard. Briony felt even more idiotic than she'd sounded because now she wanted to reach up and smooth away that frown. Oh, help! she thought.

All I've done is bump into a stranger in the rain and everything's twice as complicated as it was before. I don't need this. I need—— Suddenly, though, she no longer knew what she needed.

Perhaps he read her distress on her face, because his own expression softened. The frown that had been teasing her disappeared. He turned her towards the restaurant and said, 'Come and tell me all about it over lunch. It's the least I can offer after nearly knocking you down.'

Lunch with this man. It sounded so tempting, so deliciously tempting, that Briony had to pull back. 'You don't owe me anything,' she protested.

He did pause, but he didn't loosen his grip on her arm. 'Are you meeting your fiancé somewhere?'

'No,' she replied, incurably honest, 'but——'

'Friends?' he broke in.

'No,' she replied again, nettled that he wouldn't give her time to answer properly. 'I'm here on my own, but——'

'That settles it, then.' Decisively he steered her through the door and into the restaurant. 'You're much too young and vulnerable to be wandering around Paris by yourself.' In the foyer he slid back the hood from her hair and added, 'Much too lovely, as well.'

His directness took her breath away. So did the assured way he began to unbutton her wet coat. With all the familiarity of a lover! A lover. . . Briony was shocked by the way her thoughts were turning, and weakened as her body quivered to his touch.

She had to stop this. Now, before this stranger assumed altogether too much. And yet. . .and yet. . . As Briony hesitated a waiter came hurrying up and the chance to escape without fuss had passed. She had never in her entire life willingly caused a scene.

She suspected this handsome stranger had guessed as much, and she whispered angrily, 'You're unscrupulous!'

'No, desperate,' he murmured back. 'All my instincts tell me to hang on to you. Prove my instincts wrong over lunch and I'll let you go. I can't be fairer than that, can I?'

'I don't know. . .' she worried.

'Trust me.'

Briony was left to think about that as he turned to hand their wet coats to the waiter. They seemed to know each other, but again the conversation was too fast for her to follow. She looked about her, noting the plushy but discreet elegance of the restaurant. It was the sort of place she'd already learned to avoid, knowing a simple coffee would cost around two pounds a cup.

She looked back at the stranger who had all but forced her in here. 'Trust me,' he had said. That was a tall order, but she was willing to bet they would be shown to the best available table. Just by looking at him she knew he was the sort of man who always got what he wanted. A taxi in the rain. . .a girl in his bed. . .

Her thoughts were running away with her again. Briony gave her head a slight shake in despair, and the movement caught his attention. His hand came under her arm—that gently insistent touch—and then he was guiding her into the restaurant proper.

It was not much past midday, but it was already very full. Smart men, expensively clothed women—and me, thought Briony, in my jeans, boots and a sweater that had seen better days. She felt painfully conspicuous, and then she realised that just being with this man gave her a certain cachet. A wry smile touched her lips. Feeling desperately insecure, she was clutching at straws.

The waiter led them to a corner table overlooking the rain-washed boulevard, the very table she would have picked herself if she'd been given a free choice. It was the stranger who seated her, though, before going round the table and folding his long lean frame into the chair opposite hers. The waiter put a thick leather-bound menu in front of each of them and went away.

'Well, you've got me here, although I'm not sure how,' Briony said conversationally in an attempt to conceal how uneasy she really felt. 'Are you always this much of a bully?'

'Only when I'm frightened,' he replied with a seriousness that made her look sceptically at him.

Her eyes dwelt on the powerful shoulders not quite concealed by his well-cut suit, and she retorted, 'What could you possibly be frightened of?'

'Losing you.'

Briony caught her breath. Again that devastating directness, that frank look in his eyes that told her he wasn't afraid of what was happening between them, even if she was. She said quickly, 'Don't! Please don't flirt with me. I haven't come to Paris for a—a tatty adventure.'

'I never supposed you had.'

'Oh.' She was confused again. 'Then why——?' She couldn't go on, too afraid of making a fool of herself. Perhaps she was being over-sensitive and reading more into this than was intended.

He answered the question she hadn't asked by saying, 'I hate lunching alone, so the chance of a charming companion was too good to be missed. If I seemed a bit heavy-handed, I'm sorry, but I don't think a meal in a respectable restaurant qualifies as a tatty adventure, do you?'

'Not when you put it like that, no, but——'

'Good,' he broke in. 'Now that's sorted out perhaps we can introduce ourselves. It's long overdue. I'm Paul Deverill.'

Briony felt she was being side-tracked. She wasn't such a country hick that she couldn't spot a smooth operator when she was confronted with one, and yet he was right—nothing could be safer than this chic restaurant in the best part of Paris. In her mundane existence it qualified as an adventure, but not tatty. Not yet, anyway.

'I'm still waiting to hear your name,' Paul Deverill prompted gently.

'Briony Spenser.'

'Briony.' He repeated her name in a way that made it sound musical, special. 'How do you do, Briony?' he said, stretching his hand across the table to her, his smile inviting her to smile back.

She did, she just couldn't help herself. She placed her hand in his, and as he clasped it she felt once more that delicious sense of being protected, no longer alone. First he shook her hand and then he raised it to his lips and kissed her fingers.

That was cheating, she thought, withdrawing her hand quickly as an excited tingle ran up her arm. 'What are you, French or English?' she demanded. 'As soon as I decide you're one thing, you become another.'

'I'm English, but I grew up Channel-hopping. My grandmother was French and I spent a lot of time in Paris with her when my parents were away. They're semi-retired now, but they're journalists and do a lot of globe-trotting. My grandmother died three years ago, but we've kept on her apartment. My sister Chantal is living in it at the moment. She's a model.'

'And you?' Briony asked.

'I'm a journalist. I work for my father's company, Universal Press.'

Briony had heard of the international news agency, and she felt a tug of regret. She and Paul lived in different worlds. His was so cosmopolitan, so exciting—and out of her league.

'That's me trumped,' she replied frankly, seeing no sense in beating about the bush. 'I'm a trainee hotel manager, which so far is only a very grand way of saying I'm a receptionist. I got a year's contract with Dabell's Hotel in Kensington when I finished my college course. That ends soon and I have to make way for another student. My room goes with the job, so I should really be spending this leave job- and flat-hunting. Instead——'

Briony broke off, surprised at how much her tongue had run away with her. There was something about Paul that invited confidences. She supposed it was because he was a newsman and had the technique.

'Instead you came to Paris,' he finished for her. 'Why?'

She avoided his clear grey eyes and looked out at the boulevard. The downpour had been too torrential to last long, and already pale sunshine was shining across the wet paving. Those who had scattered when the rain started were reappearing. If her path had crossed with Paul's now, they might never have noticed each other. There were just too many people about. Strange, that.

'Why?' he insisted.

Briony looked back at him, thought of all the reasons that were not really good reasons, and shrugged. 'An impulse,' she said. 'Just a crazy impulse.'

Paul raised his hand to summon the wine waiter. 'Let's drink to impulses, the crazier the better.'

She wanted to protest and point out that she was a cautious person and not normally impulsive, but Paul was already ordering. She caught the word 'champagne'. Perhaps there was something magical about it, because all urge to protest faded. A delightful feeling of irresponsibility crept over her.

It was Paul's influence, of course, but a stolen hour of pleasure no longer seemed the crime of the century. Matthew wouldn't know about it, so he couldn't suffer for it. And she—she would be able to push aside her cares, and probably be all the better for it.

The wine waiter went away, and Paul opened his

menu. 'Time we ordered,' he said. 'Do you need any help with the French?'

Briony shook her head. 'I've been moonlighting as a waitress in a French restaurant for extra cash.'

'To come to Paris?' he asked.

'No, to get married,' she corrected.

'I'm sorry I asked that.'

His grimace made Briony smile as she opened her own menu. She flicked through the pages, scanning the prices first. They were exorbitant, as she'd expected. She raised troubled brown eyes to his and said with difficulty, 'I feel I should pay for my own meal, but frankly I can't. This would blow my budget for the rest of the week.'

'It won't blow mine, and you're my guest. If you're frightened of being under some sort of obligation, forget it. You're doing me a favour. I told you, I hate lunching alone,' Paul reassured her, then changed the subject. 'I can recommend the *aubergines fourrées* as a starter, unless you'd like something lighter.'

'I think so,' Briony replied. 'I'm not used to eating at midday. I usually have a good evening meal and skip lunch altogether.'

'Not with me you don't,' he said bluntly, flicking over another page. 'What about the *melon à l'orange*?'

'I was just looking at that. Yes, that will do nicely.'

'And for the main course?' he asked.

'*Homard Thermidor*,' she replied, abandoning caution and going overboard completely. Lobster and champagne—when would she have the chance to eat so sumptuously again? Probably not for years.

She waited for a twinge of guilt about Matthew to mar her light spirits, but nothing happened. Even her conscience seemed to have accepted that this was just an hour of fantasy, and real life wouldn't begin again until it was over.

This wasn't really her, Briony Spenser. This was another creature who didn't really exist. But oh, it was so good to be somebody else for a little while— and, so long as nobody was hurt, what harm could it possiby do?

Paul decided, 'I'll join you in the lobster but stick with the aubergines to start with.' He closed his menu and the waiter, watching him, arrived to take their order. As he went away, the champagne arrived.

When the ritual of popping the cork and filling the glasses had been gone through, the wine waiter nestled the bottle into its bucket of ice and left them alone. Paul raised his glass and toasted, 'To impulses.'

'To impulses,' she repeated, smiling, and they both drank. She wrinkled her nose at the bubbles, but that was part of the ritual too, and when she saw Paul looking at her her smile widened.

'That's better, you're relaxing at last,' he approved.

'I can't help it. Champagne makes me feel so spoiled.'

'It suits you. You should be spoiled more often. The colour is back in your cheeks. You remind me of a rose unfurling its petals and getting lovelier all the time.'

Briony turned pink with pleasure, then he continued, 'And just in case you think I'm flirting with you and go all hostile on me again, I'll propose another toast—to your wedding.'

She came down to earth with a jolt she couldn't quite explain away to herself. She'd made it clear enough she was spoken for, so why should she feel this searing, aching regret that he'd taken her at her word? It was nonsensical.

'Don't you want to drink to your wedding, Briony?' Paul asked quietly.

'Yes—yes, of course.' She raised her glass and drank so hastily that she choked.

Paul drank too, but more slowly, his eyes never leaving her face. He was about to say something when the first course arrived, and it wasn't until they were halfway through it that he asked, 'Can we unravel the mystery now?'

Briony raised her eyes from her slices of melon, appetisingly presented with thin strips of fresh orange, and stared at him. 'What mystery?'

'You.'

The word hung on the air between them, then she laughed. 'Me? You must be kidding! I'm the least mysterious of people.'

'Not to me.' Paul leaned his elbows on the table and began to tick off points on his fingers. 'One, you only think you're getting married soon. Two, you blow some of your wedding savings on coming to Paris by yourself. Three, you explain it away as an impulse. I'm all for that but, four, it isn't the sort of impulse a bride-to-be normally has. If that's not mysterious, what is?'

'It does seem a bit odd, put like that,' she admitted.

Paul finished his aubergine, but when she didn't elaborate he suggested, 'Wedding nerves, Briony?'

'I—I suppose so.' She hated admitting it, it seemed so disloyal. She finished her melon and, as soon as the first course was cleared and the second served, she added, 'I wouldn't like you to get the wrong idea. No two people could be more right for each other than Matthew and I. I just need a little time to get myself sorted out, readjust to a new situation.'

She sounded, she thought disgustedly, like an emotionally immature teenager. A sophisticated man like Paul Deverill must be regretting that he'd got himself involved. As though he'd picked up her thoughts, he asked, 'How old are you, Briony?'

'Twenty-one.'

'You don't look it.'

'You mean I don't sound it,' she scoffed.

'I didn't say that.'

'You didn't have to, but I'm more than old enough to know my own mind, and usually I do.' Briony wrinkled her forehead in an effort to explain. 'Matthew—my fiancé—sent me a cable and it knocked me off balance. It was so unexpected, so unlike him, I couldn't seem to think straight. I suppose I was in a little bit of a panic, really. I thought if only I could get away from everything for a little while I'd be able to think properly, get everything into perspective. That's why I'm in Paris.'

Briony, fishing a slice of mushroom from the sauce covering her lobster and eating it, thought she must sound more inane than ever and wished she'd held her tongue. There didn't seem any way she could explain how unlike herself this was, and that normally she was the most level-headed person going.

'When did you get this cable?' Paul asked.

'Thursday.'

His dark eyebrows rose. 'When did you come to Paris?'

'Saturday.'

'That sounds like more than a little bit of a panic to me,' he said drily. 'What did this cable say that was so startling?'

'That he's coming home next Saturday and wants us to get married right away. He's in the States and wasn't due home until July, and this is only the beginning of March. It should have been a lovely surprise, but suddenly I didn't feel—ready. I didn't know why and so I. . .' Her voice trailed away, her uncertainties refusing to be pinned down to words.

'And so you ran away,' Paul finished for her. 'All the way to Paris.'

'I wouldn't put it that strongly,' Briony objected. 'I went into the travel agent's to book a few days in Brighton or somewhere like that; while I was there, somebody cancelled this Paris trip. It's the last week of winter prices, so it was cheap, with bed, breakfast and travel all included. The next thing I knew, I was booking it. As I said, it was an impulse thing.'

Paul had finished his lobster and was leaning back in his chair studying her thoughtfully. 'You do know,' he said after a while, 'that wedding nerves mean wedding doubts.'

'Yes, I know,' she replied, putting down her own

knife and fork. 'I'm also still certain Matthew and I are absolutely right for each other.'

'No, you're not, or you wouldn't have fled to Paris.'

'I haven't fled anywhere,' Briony returned heatedly. 'At least, if I have—oh, you just don't know the situation!'

Paul smiled suddenly, charmingly, and said with that devastating directness she was beginning to dread, 'I think I know enough of the situation between you and Matthew by now to turn it to my advantage.'

'Y-your advantage?' Briony stuttered.

'Yes.' He lifted the champagne bottle from its nest of ice and refilled her glass. 'This seems as good a moment as any for confessing that I had an ulterior motive for inviting you to lunch.'

'An—an ulterior motive?' she faltered, wishing she could stop stammering and repeating things like a parrot.

'That's what I said.' Paul raised his glass and toasted, 'To us, Briony. Just for one night.'

# CHAPTER TWO

PAUL drank, but Briony didn't touch her glass. 'If that's your idea of a joke, it's not mine. I don't play around,' she said angrily.

'Half a night, then,' he bargained, not the least bit penitent.

'No! Lunch is as far as you and I go.'

'Afraid you might enjoy yourself?' he suggested.

'Certainly not!'

'I think you are. You've come all the way to Paris to figure out whether you're ready to marry. It's a bit of a wasted effort if you haven't the courage to put your doubts to the test.'

Briony was silent, wondering how Paul managed to make what was wrong sound so reasonable. Finally she asked, 'What sort of a test?'

'My sister's having a little going-away party tonight. She's off to the Bahamas for ten days to model beachwear. I want you to come. If you enjoy yourself with me, you'll know Matthew isn't exactly vital to your life.' Paul paused, then added purposefully, 'If he isn't, don't marry him, because one day you'll meet somebody who is.'

It made a funny sort of sense, but Briony asked suspiciously, 'What's in it for you?'

'A pretty girl to take to a party. I'm at a loose end in Paris, the same as you.'

'Oh.' That was a surprise, but she didn't have time

to follow it through, because the waiter swooped to clear away the main course.

'What would you like for sweet?' Paul asked.

'I'll skip it, thanks. I couldn't eat another thing.'

He spoke to the waiter and, when they were alone again, Briony said, 'I thought you were working in Paris for the news agency.'

'No. I've been in Israel for two years and I'm at the tail-end of a leave before I fly out to Hong Kong.'

Hong Kong. . .the other side of the world. Briony found she didn't like to think of him so far away, which was ridiculous. 'For very long?' she asked.

'Only three months. I'll be managing the bureau while the regular fellow takes an extended holiday.'

'And then?'

'I'll be taking over the New York bureau for two years.' Paul gave her another of his disconcertingly intent looks, then said, 'Today's Sunday and I fly to Hong Kong first thing Saturday morning. How about you?'

'I go home on Saturday as well.'

'Nothing could be more convenient, then, could it? We both have five days to fill in, so we might as well fill them in together. I could show you Paris, and you could save me from my sister's attempts to pair me off with one of her friends. I'm sure that's what this farewell party is all about tonight and, frankly, I prefer to find my own women.'

'Yes, but I'm not one of your women,' Briony bridled.

'She's not to know that, is she?'

Briony had the feeling something wasn't quite

right, but while she was trying to put her finger on exactly what the waiter returned, put a stemmed dessert dish in front of each of them and went away. 'I didn't order anything,' she protested.

'I ordered for you. The caramel cream here takes some beating. It will slide down without your even noticing,' Paul coaxed.

'I don't know why you even bother to consult me. You do exactly what you want, anyway,' she grumbled, but she tasted the caramel cream, and it was delicious. It was served with sweet biscuits rolled up like brandy snaps, and she found herself nibbling one of those as well. 'This party,' she mused, 'will there be many people there?'

'With Chantal there's no telling, but probably. The only thing I can promise is that it'll be fun.'

'Your idea of fun and mine might be different,' she hedged.

'I'll take you back to your hotel the minute you ask me to,' Paul promised. 'Where is your hotel, by the way?'

Briony, having got the taste for the caramel cream, began to eat it. 'It's a walk-up not far from the Avenue de la République on the east side of Paris. The Hotel Marie-Louise.'

'I'll pick you up at eight.'

'Hey! I haven't said I'll go yet,' she objected.

'Briony, you can't tell me it's much fun wandering around a strange city by yourself, specially when you don't speak the language.'

'No,' she admitted, thinking how lonely and miserable she'd been after only a day—and how nervous of straying by mistake into a rough area. It would have been different if she was a naturally assertive person, but she wasn't, and a deep-rooted insecurity made her terrified of making a fool of herself.

'You don't find me hard to get along with, do you?' Paul persisted.

She stole a shy glance at him and admitted again, 'No.'

'Then come to the party with me tonight. See how you get on. You can make up your mind afterwards whether or not you'd like me to show you around Paris.'

He seemed so sure she'd have no further objections that she found herself agreeing, 'All right, but I haven't brought any party clothes. I just threw a few things into a travelling-bag more or less on the basis of what came first. I was working until late Friday evening. I had to get a Euro-passport and change up some currency during my lunch break because I was off first thing Saturday morning. There wasn't time to think, just act.'

'That's the way I live my life,' Paul murmured. 'Would you like to drink another toast to impulses?'

Briony shook her head. 'No, thanks. I'll be forgetting the traffic drives on the wrong side of the road and walking under a bus, but don't let me stop you.'

'No, I'm driving. Chantal isn't using her car today, so I commandeered it.'

'Like you commandeered me?' she suggested.

'No, she's much more persuadable, being my kid sister. As for the party, wear anything you like. It will be strictly casual. Chantal has enough of dressing up when she's working.' Paul caught the waiter's eye and ordered coffee.

While they were drinking it, he said, 'You're not wearing an engagement ring.'

Briony looked down at the bare third finger on her left hand and shrugged. 'Call it a cash-flow problem. When Matthew and I became engaged we were living precariously on student grants eked out by doing casual work during holidays. A ring wasn't important to us. The big thing was deciding we belonged together, being the way we are. Your life has been so different from ours, you wouldn't understand.'

'Try me,' Paul suggested, leaning across and covering her hand with his. It was a brief, reassuring touch, and when he straightened up he said, 'Start by explaining what you mean by "the way we are".'

Briony didn't know whether it was because he was so easy to talk to, or simply because the need to confide in somebody was overwhelming, but she found herself saying, 'We both had disrupted childhoods. My parents were killed in a road crash. Matthew's split up and didn't want him, so we both grew up the same way—sometimes in children's homes, sometimes being fostered out, but never feeling we belonged anywhere or to anyone. It made us loners, cautious, afraid of giving or receiving affection in case it didn't last.' She broke off and gave a self-conscious laugh. 'Please stop me if I'm boring you to death.'

'I wouldn't be here if you were. I'm not the long-suffering type,' Paul replied. 'Where did you grow up?'

'Norfolk. I moved into Norwich to take my hotel management course at technical college. I got a room in a house shared by four university students. Matthew was one of them. He's frightfully brainy. He was a second-year student, reading physics. I didn't see much of him, but I didn't know then it was because he was a loner like me. I'd always thought I was the only misfit around.'

Paul beckoned the waiter to pour more coffee, then said, 'I wouldn't call you a misfit, or anything like it.'

Briony smiled. 'I'm never going to be a raving extrovert, but I'm much less defensive now, and that's thanks to Matthew. You see, during my second term at college I went down with glandular fever. Matthew looked after me. I had to drop out of college and it was months before I was well again. Heaven knows what I'd have done without him, because I couldn't have coped by myself. He took care of everything, even arranging for me to restart my studies when the new college year began.'

She paused and looked out at the boulevard without seeing anything, just remembering. Almost to herself, she continued, 'When I was well again life was different. I wasn't lonely any more. I had a companion, a friend I cared about and who cared about me. Gradually that bond deepened. We understood and trusted each other, which was a pretty big thing for both of us. We'd neither of us had anybody we could depend on before. We just sort of knew we belonged together without ever having to put it into words.'

Paul, stirring his coffee, said wryly, 'You must have put it into words some time. You got engaged.'

'That was almost at the end of our last terms.'

Briony flushed slightly and went on, 'We were so much a part of each other's lives by then that we became engaged and lived together. It was wonderful, really belonging to someone, then we graduated. I got my diploma. Matthew passed his degree with honours and then—then we had to split up. He's so brilliant he was offered this marvellous chance to take his Masters in the States, all expenses paid by a Californian company that wanted him to work for them afterwards.'

'Why didn't you go with him?' Paul asked.

'I couldn't afford to. I took the job I was offered in London and started saving. Matthew was coming home in July. We were going to marry and go to California together. Then out of the blue I got this cable to say he's returning to marry me right away.'

'Very romantic,' he observed drily. 'You should be over the moon.'

'I know, but it's so unlike him. Matthew is—is *steady*. He plans things, and he doesn't suddenly turn everything upside-down without an explanation. I'm afraid something's gone terribly wrong for him, but there hasn't been a hint of anything in his letters.'

'What interests me more,' Paul said bluntly, 'is finding out what has gone wrong for you.'

Briony bit her lip and her brown eyes slid away from his. 'I'm not sure anything has.'

'Now you're being evasive.'

'Not deliberately,' she protested. 'I'm just so muddled. I don't for a moment doubt that Matthew and I belong together. At the same time, I know I'm not the same person I was a year ago. Working in

London has changed me. I love my work, I've made friends, I've learned to cope with situations that would have frightened me before. It's all because Matthew gave me a—a security I never had. I owe him so much, and yet——'

'You don't owe him your whole life,' Paul broke in brutally. 'That's what you're afraid to put into words, isn't it?'

She shook her head violently. 'No! I knew you wouldn't understand. Nobody could.'

Silence fell between them. She knew Paul was looking at her in that assessing way of his, but she refused to meet his eyes. Eventually he said, 'All right, have it your way. I don't understand. I could tell you what I *think*, but I'm not going to get my head bitten off again.'

Against her will, Briony looked at him. He was smiling at her so quizzically that she softened and borrowed one of his expressions. 'Try me,' she suggested.

He laughed. 'I'll say one thing for you, you learn fast!'

She was pleased because she felt she had his approval, and that meant more than she cared to admit. 'Is that what you were thinking?' she asked, knowing very well that it wasn't, but unable to resist teasing him.

'What I was thinking, Briony, won't amuse you.'

She lost her nerve and said hastily, 'Don't tell me, then.'

'I won't. Not until I think you're ready for it.'

Perversely, she was irritated and snapped, 'I might never be.'

'That's a risk I have to take.'

She wanted to ask him what he meant by that, but Paul was signalling the waiter for the bill. She felt snubbed, and was hurt, but she supposed it was her own fault. Paul must have got a lot more than he bargained for when he shanghaied her for lunch. She should never have tried to explain things that couldn't be explained, only felt. . .

She felt like a schoolgirl again, insecure, awkward, untidy and not quite up to standard. Not at all the sort of female Paul would want to be associated with. She felt it only fair to let him off the hook, quite forgetting in her dismay that he had made all the running.

As she gathered her shoulder-bag and gloves and began to rise, she said, 'Look, I think it was a mistake to invite me to your sister's party tonight and——'

'I don't make mistakes,' he broke in positively, 'and I mean to make sure you don't either.'

He settled the bill, came around the table and took her arm. Briony's head was in a whirl as he collected their raincoats and led her out of the restaurant. She no longer knew what to think. She'd never met anybody like Paul before. Things happened so fast with him. She wondered if he was always like this, or whether he was deliberately making sure she had no time to sort out what she really thought and felt.

When they were under the awning outside the restaurant once more, he asked, 'Do you want to wear your raincoat?'

'No.' In her confused state, she was glad of

something normal to talk about. The sunshine that had followed the rain was weak, but it wasn't cold. She took the coat from him and put it over her arm.

'Where were you going when we met? I could drop you off there,' Paul said.

For some peculiar reason, Briony was disappointed that he didn't mean to follow through his offer to show her Paris right away. She knew she had no right to be, but that didn't stop her feeling hurt again. That triggered off her defensive mechanism. She wasn't going to hold him a minute longer than necessary if he had better things to do.

'Thanks, but I don't need a lift,' she replied. 'My sightseeing this afternoon is better done on foot. I'm going to stroll down the Champs-Elysées to the Place de la Concorde and maybe look in at the Louvre.'

Paul slid up the left sleeve of her red sweater and looked at the neat watch strapped to her wrist. 'Keep your eye on that,' he ordered. 'Somebody once worked out that if you spent just four seconds in front of every masterpiece in the Louvre it would still take you four months to see them all—and you don't have that much time. I'm picking you up at eight, on the dot.' His big strong hand came up and touched her face. 'Take care,' he said, then he was striding across the wide boulevard to the low-slung red sports car parked at the kerb.

Briony walked on in a daze. His touch had been light, but she could still feel the imprint of his hand on her face. It had been tender, almost a caress. A lover's touch, her heart whispered, but her brain refused to believe it. She didn't know where she kept getting this funny feeling that Paul was claiming her for his own, when he'd made it clear enough what his interest in her was.

A companion for lunch because he hated lunching alone. A friend to take to a party to fend off his sister's matchmaking attempts. It made sense if he didn't want to get deeply involved with anybody during the short time he was in Paris. She would be going home soon to marry Matthew, her doubts mastered and overcome. Paul would feel safe with her, and she would feel safe with him.

Wouldn't she?

Briony, uneasy yet filled with the strange excitement Paul generated in her, walked along the most famous avenue in Paris without taking in a thing. She certainly looked at all the enticing shops, but nothing really registered. She was too absorbed in coming to terms with what had happened to her since she'd met Paul.

Her hour of fantasy hadn't ended. She was still caught up in it. Briony tried to tell herself she'd met a handsome, exciting man who was manipulating her for his own purposes, but it was no use. She just wasn't in the mood for common sense. She was being offered the chance to escape from reality for a little while, and she was going to grab it. It might not be like her, but when had she ever liked herself, anyway?

Real life would intrude again soon enough. . .

A display of handbags in one of the boutique windows caught Briony's eye because it was backed by mirrors. She paused to look at herself, puzzled why she should have caught Paul's attention. There were so many more attractively dressed women around.

But not in the rain, she reminded herself. There hadn't been any competition then. She was sure he wouldn't have noticed her if there had been. It was a long, long time since she'd looked at herself from a man's point of view. She was expecting a drab, rather uninspiring reflection, and she was surprised. Her clothes might be well worn and casual, but she was slender enough to wear them with a certain air, and just tall enough to look almost elegant. But it was her face that surprised her the most. There was a glow about it, some unknown force that came from within, that matched how she felt—a different Briony Spenser altogether.

Had she once looked like that for Matthew? And would she again? She supposed so, when she returned to England and normality. Whatever happened to her in Paris, and whatever her doubts about the future, she couldn't imagine its having any long-term effect on the bond between her and Matthew.

Briony knew this was as good a time as any to really think things through, but her mind refused to co-operate. She was developing a taste for being out of touch with reality, and that was what a holiday was all about, wasn't it? This different, more adventurous Briony would have such a short lease of life that it seemed a pity to weigh her down with past or future problems.

She walked on, feeling more light-hearted with each step. She tried to tell herself it was the champagne, but she knew it wasn't. It was Paul. Well, she wasn't going to worry about that either. At some point she would measure him up against Matthew and find him wanting.

When that happened she could go back to England and give herself to Matthew as freely and happily as she had last summer, all questions answered and all doubts resolved. Having come to that conclusion, she didn't think about Matthew again.

For reasons of his own, Paul had challenged her to put her feelings to the test. For reasons of her own, she'd accepted. It was only now, though, that she felt ready to see it through. Ready and eager. . .

# CHAPTER THREE

BRIONY arrived at the Place de la Concorde just as a light drizzle began, nothing to be compared with the earlier downpour. She put on her raincoat and looked about her. She was normally imaginative, and she'd read her guidebook well, but not for the life of her could she imagine the scene when heads had rolled under the guillotine set up in this vast square during the Revolution two hundred years before.

She was too much in the present, and all her senses were tuned in to Paul. She looked at her watch. There were several hours to go before she saw him again, but she decided to skip going on to the Louvre. It would only tire her, and she'd had precious little sleep since receiving Matthew's cable.

Suddenly the prospect of going back to the hotel seemed more attractive than any sightseeing. She could rest, ponder what she was going to wear that evening, then lash out on a bath. There was only a washbasin in her room and a bath was extra, but because she'd done so much walking and Paul had bought her lunch, she'd spent nowhere near the ten pounds a day she was trying to live on.

Not that she did care whether she blew her budget, she was so buoyed up on excitement and anticipation. The Concorde Métro was close by, and she'd already discovered how quick and cheap it was to travel around Paris by underground. She went down, changed trains twice, and as she was walking towards the exit close to her hotel she passed a stall laden with junk jewellery.

She was wearing tiny gold studs in her ears, Matthew's parting present to her, but she paused and studied the barbaric drop earrings on display. Perhaps a pair would give her a new touch, be more in keeping with her more adventurous self.

In answer to her tentative, '*Combien*?' she discovered they were very cheap. She selected a pair of outrageously large pendant drops, paid for them, and walked on to her hotel, trying to make up her mind whether they were cheap and nasty or fashionable and fun. Perhaps she'd wear them, perhaps she wouldn't. She'd see how she felt when the moment came.

When she arrived at her hotel the reception desk was empty. The concierge was in a back room watching television. Briony pinged the desk bell and he came into the foyer, all smiles and chatting volubly. Briony, scarcely understanding one word in ten, hoped her answering smile was reply enough.

She took her key and began to walk up the stairs that twisted and turned about a central stairway. The hotel rambled over eight identical floors, but she was lucky, her room was at the end of a corridor on the second storey.

She went in, locked the door behind her and walked over to the long french window that overlooked a factory car park. The wild cats that lived there fascinated her. They emerged from nowhere as the cars arrived in the morning and leapt on to the engine-warmed bonnets to sleep off a cold night's roaming. Today, though, the rain had driven the cats under the cars and there was nothing for her to watch.

Briony, yawning, could only assume there was some sort of production emergency in the factory to bring the workers in on a Sunday, and she wondered where the cats slept when the car park was empty. Then she yawned again, giving into an exhaustion that was as much emotional as physical, and swished the curtains closed.

A glance at her watch showed it was three-thirty. She had plenty of time. She removed her sweater, pulled off her boots and lay down on top of the narrow bed to rest and relive all that she'd said to Paul and, more importantly, all that he'd said to her. Her eyes closed, fluttered open and closed again. They stayed closed until a burst of laughter and the slamming of a door further along the corridor awoke her.

For a moment she lay unmoving. The central heating was so efficient it made the small room stuffy, and she'd slept so deeply she felt stupefied. She got up slowly and wandered over to the window to let some fresh air into the room. The car park was empty of cars or cats. The workers must have gone home, and presumably the cats had vanished on another night's marauding. They must find rich pickings. They all looked sleek and well fed.

*Night's marauding?* Briony, leaning against the small wardrobe adjacent to the window and yawning away the heaviness of an afternoon's sleep, snapped upright into alertness. Grief, whatever was the time?

She focused on her watch and breathed a little easier, but only a little. In just two hours Paul would be here, and she'd forgotten to book a bathroom. She threw on her dressing-gown and slippers, grabbed her washbag and a couple of bottles from the shelf above the washbasin, and hurried down to Reception. She was in luck—there was a bathroom vacant.

She soaked in perfumed water, shampooed her hair under the shower attachment and went back up to her room feeling tinglingly alive. She plugged in her hair-drier and brushed her long hair into gleaming submission as it dried, scarcely able to contain the excitement mounting within her as the minutes ticked by.

There seemed to be a barrier between herself and feelings of guilt about Matthew. They were there, but they really didn't get through to her. It was as though her conscience had so thoroughly accepted Paul as somebody outside her real life that she wasn't answerable for her actions.

She had escaped from herself, and the recklessness that engendered was too heady to resist.

It was almost eight o'clock as she flung a last hasty look at herself in the mirror. Again, she scarcely recognised the vital creature reflected there, and yet this black jersey dress was scarcely new. It was a long tube style and she'd belted it at the hips to raise it a few inches above her ankles. The sleeves were elbow-length and the neck was slightly cut away to show the graceful line of her neck and just a suggestion of her shoulders.

Her hairstyle was scarcely revolutionary either—

two narrow plaits at her temples brought round to the back to tie over the rest of her hair, which hung loose past her shoulders. The difference in her must stem from a vitality coming from within, or maybe it was the earrings. Normally she dressed to merge with the background, but the large swinging pendants screamed for attention.

She looked like one of the vital, got-it-all-together girls she usually envied, and felt a tremor of misgiving, doubting whether she had the personality to back up her appearance. It was too late for doubts, though, so she swung the strap of her bag over her shoulder and threw her raincoat over her arm. She hadn't packed any evening accessories, not thinking she would need them, and she just had to make do with what she had.

There were a lot of people on the stairs, presumably all making their way out for dinner. The hotel provided a sparse Continental breakfast and no other meals at all. Briony hurried past them, and it was only as she was on the last flight of stairs that she slowed down.

She'd just thought how awful it would be if she burst into the foyer and Paul wasn't there to meet her. She'd look such a fool, rushing for nothing. Her old apprehension clouded her dark eyes as she went down the last of the steps and looked around, and then everything was all right. Paul was rising from one of the armchairs and coming across to meet her.

She relaxed and a spontaneous smile of welcome glowed over her face. It warmed Paul, who was used to more guile. He was wearing a loose-knit cream sweater over brown trousers and looked every bit as handsome as he had in his tailored suit. 'You look beautiful,' he said simply.

It was what Briony needed to be told, and her glow deepened, but modesty made her say, 'Thank you, but I think that's a bit of an exaggeration.'

'You think a lot of funny things,' he replied, taking her arm and leading her outside. 'I shall have to see what I can do about that.'

It was a fine evening, just a little chilly, and she was debating whether to throw her coat around her shoulders when she saw his sister's sports car parked right outside the hotel. She felt very special as Paul handed her into it and, with a little sigh of pleasure, she gave herself up once more to the fantasy world he created for her.

'What was that sigh for?' Paul asked as he eased the car into the traffic.

'I feel like somebody else,' she confessed. 'It's fun. . .for a little while.'

'How long is "a little while"?' As soon as he'd said it, he added, 'No, don't answer that. Fun shouldn't be pinned into hours or days. It might spoil it.'

This was so much in tune with her own feelings that Briony caught her breath, surprised there should be such an instinctive understanding between them. She asked with a smile, 'Are you sure you're a newsman and not a poet?'

He laughed, and she was ridiculously pleased with herself for amusing him. 'I'm very sure,' he replied. 'I deal in hard facts. The dreams I leave to others.'

Her smile faded and she didn't answer. 'Have I said something wrong?' Paul asked, giving her a long and considering look as he stopped at traffic-lights.

'No,' she lied, not even sure why she was lying. 'I was just wondering where your sister lived.'

Apparently he decided to accept the clumsy change of subject, because as the lights changed he answered, 'The Ile St-Louis. Five bridges connect it with the right and left banks of the Seine, but it's still one of the most peaceful parts of the city.'

She summoned up a mental picture of the map she carried in her shoulder-bag, and ventured, 'You mean where Notre Dame is?'

'No, you're thinking of the larger island, the Ile de la Cité. Paris was founded there and it's a prime tourist target. The Ile St-Louis, or l'Ile, as it's known, is more residential. My grandmother was born there. My grandfather carried her off to England, but she returned when he died. My sister Chantal must be a throwback to her. She's more at home in Paris than anywhere else.'

'And you?' Briony asked.

'I'm not fussy. I like living out of a suitcase.'

'I can't imagine anybody living like that from choice. My dream has always been a settled home,' she said wistfully.

'That's because you've never had one.'

'I suppose so.' Unwelcome reality intruded as she realised how very different she and Paul were, and she went on with forced lightness, 'We're chalk and cheese, aren't we?'

'We're Paul and Briony,' he corrected. 'A bit more interesting, I hope.' She laughed, and he said approvingly, 'That's better. I was beginning to think too much walking around this afternoon had worn you out.'

'I cheated. I skipped the Louvre, went back to my hotel and surprised myself by falling asleep. I ended up in a frantic rush.'

'I live in a rush,' Paul replied, crossing the night-quiet river by a sturdily arched bridge. 'It beats sitting around waiting for things to happen.'

*Definitely* chalk and cheese, Briony thought. The only positive action she'd ever taken was this trip to Paris. Everything else in her life had just sort of happened to her.

Paul broke into her thoughts by pulling up and saying, 'Here we are.'

She looked out. They were parked on a *quai*, tree-lined on the river side. On the other side were tall, flat-fronted mansions. The one they were parked outside stretched over five floors with a quaintly gabled roof. Ornate balconies decorated the shuttered windows, and Briony breathed, 'It looks very grand.'

'This is a fragment of the old, aristocratic Paris that has survived more or less intact,' he told her, smiling. 'It had the good fortune not to be in the way when the boulevards and squares were carved into the city. This particular house is broken into apartments, but we're lucky enough to have the top two floors. My grandmother always maintained that it's easy to breathe up there, even in August when it's so hot.'

He ushered her under a narrow stone archway, unlocked a heavy door and walked her through an elegant hall to a gilded cage of a lift. 'I feel like a canary,' she said, as he closed the door and pressed a button.

He laughed. 'You can sing if you like. The acoustics should be pretty good. This place was built of stone to last.'

She didn't feel like singing or even smiling. The lift had stopped, and the prospect of socialising with a lot of strangers pitchforked her back into her old insecure self. She bit her lip and said anxiously, 'What if I can't understand a word anybody's saying? I'll feel such a dummy.'

'But a lovely dummy,' he teased.

'It's not funny. I'll be all fingers and thumbs.'

Paul raised her hands to his lips. 'Lovely fingers and thumbs,' he murmured, kissing each one in turn.

It was a novel, provocative experience, but Briony was too apprehensive to enjoy it. He released her hands, tipped her face up to his and frowned at the anxiety in her eyes. 'Hey,' he went on softly, 'I brought you here to enjoy yourself, not to have a nervous breakdown! You must meet strangers all the time, working in a hotel.'

'That's different. I have things to do. I'm just not very good at standing around trying to think of things to say when everybody else is being witty and clever. It's going to be twice as bad when I can't even understand the language.'

'You're worrying about nothing,' Paul told her. 'This is a pretty cosmopolitan bunch. A few are English, and those who aren't speak the language. I wouldn't have brought you if I didn't think you'd fit in.'

'Thank you, but I'm not at all cosmopolitan. I'm——'

'You're the girl I wanted to bring to the party,' he

broke in. 'That should tell you something.' He kissed her very gently on the cheek and asked, 'All right now?'

She was overcome by such a swirl of conflicting emotions she couldn't speak, only nod. Part of her brain registered that Paul's motives for dating her seemed to change to suit the occasion, and yet he always had this tremendous power to reassure her. It made it impossible for her to be wary of him, even though she knew she should be.

'Paul. . .' she began uneasily.

'Yes?'

With his grey eyes looking so steadily into hers, her doubts about his determination to befriend her faded away. 'Nothing,' she replied. 'I'm fine now.'

'That's my girl,' he said with the easy camaraderie she envied so much. He slid back the lift door, opened another and led her straight into a room crowded with people.

Briony, expecting to find herself in a hallway, was taken by surprise and instinctively recoiled. She came up against Paul's arm as he slid it around her waist. She felt his warmth and strength and was instantly comforted. She threw him a grateful smile and he drew her more closely to his side. All urge to flee left her and she relaxed.

They were in a spacious drawing-room furnished with low-backed Edwardian settees and matching dainty chairs. 'How lovely!' she said spontaneously. 'Not much can have changed since your grand-mother's time.'

'It hasn't. Not to create a shrine to her or anything morbid like that, but because we couldn't better her taste. Everything suits the apartment so well we can't imagine it any other way.'

'Neither can I, and this is the first time I've seen it,' Briony replied, thinking how lucky Paul was to have such continuity in his family. She and Matthew would have to start from scratch. They had only each other.

Her thoughts were turned in another direction as a girl detached herself from a group and came towards them. She was tall, arrestingly beautiful and casually clothed in black ski-pants with a smock-like multi-coloured silk top. Briony knew she was Paul's sister. There was the same clarity in the wide grey eyes, the same richness in the brown hair, the same erect, confident carriage.

'Chantal,' he introduced.

'You must be Briony,' she said, and to Briony's surprise she clasped her lightly by the shoulders and kissed her on the cheek. As if, Briony thought confusedly, I were an old friend, or even one of the family. It made her feel special, just as Paul did.

She didn't feel at all shy as Chantal and Paul began to introduce her around. They made it so easy for her, one or the other of them always at her side. Her confidence grew, and after a while she found herself chatting as easily and naturally as everybody else, her fear of having to flounder through awkward silences completely gone.

It was an exhilarating experience, actually enjoying a party. Her eyes glowed, her cheeks were flushed and she could never remember laughing so much. Once Paul leaned close to her and murmured, 'Not so much of a lame duck, are you, Briony?'

'Quack, quack,' she replied.

Paul threw back his head and laughed. 'More petals unfurling,' he said, and pulled her head against his shoulder.

She emerged from his quick, impulsive hug even more flushed and glowing, and found herself looking straight into Chantal's speculative eyes. Her own eyebrows rose in unconscious questioning, but Chantal only smiled and turned away to speak to somebody else.

Paul was called away to another group to settle a laughing dispute, but Briony remained where she was, no longer needing him as a prop to lean on. She could manage very well by herself now, and wanted to prove it, like a child delightedly exhibiting a newly acquired skill.

She knew it was all for Paul's sake, that she wanted him to be proud of her, but she wasn't going to spoil everything by looking too deeply into that. She was always conscious, though, of where he was in the room, and something within her ached to have him back by her side. She knew that sooner or later he would be, and there was a bitter-sweet anticipation in waiting for the moment.

Somebody put on some moody music and couples began to smooch around the room, the conversation lessening as groups broke up into twos. The anticipation became unbearable as Briony waited for Paul to come and claim her. She was certain that he would, but she wasn't going to give herself away by looking over at his group.

She felt a touch on her arm and turned eagerly, then had to hide her disappointment when she saw it wasn't Paul who stood there but his sister. 'I'm going to serve up the food,' Chantal said. 'Would you like to help? We haven't had much time to chat.'

'Of course,' Briony replied, a little puzzled why she was being singled out. All at once she remembered that strangely speculative look Chantal had given her earlier. Paul's sister definitely had something on her mind.

Baffled, she began to follow her towards the kitchen when suddenly Paul's arm was around her waist, swinging her towards him. 'Listen,' he said, nodding towards the stereo. ' "Raindrops keep falling on my head". Definitely our dance.'

Chantal looked back. 'Put her down, Paul,' she joked, 'or you won't be fed!'

'The food can wait, the music can't,' he replied, pulling Briony into his arms and beginning to dance with her. Before Chantal could protest further she too was claimed and danced away from the kitchen. 'That settles it,' Paul murmured, drawing Briony closer to him as they were bumped by another couple. 'Considering the way we met, this has to be our tune.'

'Yes,' she whispered, knowing they shouldn't have their own tune or be dancing together in this way. But what she knew and what she felt were two different things, and once again it was so much easier to surrender to the mood of the moment.

There was a surge of movement by the lift door as more people arrived and greetings were exchanged, but Briony, her head hidden against Paul's chest, had her eyes closed and she didn't open them. She wanted the song to go on forever, and when it stopped she could have cried.

Paul led her over to the stereo and put it on again. They danced on, lost to the world—at least, Briony knew that she was. The second time the music stopped he put her firmly away from him. 'Briony,' he said unsmilingly, 'either you run away to the kitchen—now, this instant—or we dance ourselves into bed.'

Briony didn't need telling what he meant. She fled.

# CHAPTER FOUR

THERE was nobody in the kitchen, and Briony wasn't sorry, needing a few moments to get herself together. She was ashamed of the way her body had clung to Paul's as they danced, and yet wildly exhilarated as well. What frightened her most was that she seemed to be developing a taste for playing with fire.

This wasn't her, of course. It was the other creature who had taken possession of her ever since she'd met Paul. Matthew's Briony felt the shame and Paul's Briony the exhilaration. The problem was that she was no longer sure which of them was her real self.

She looked around, dazedly seeking a clue that would guide her. All she saw was a large kitchen that was a happy mixture of old and new—huge built-in dressers that looked as though they'd been there since the year dot, a big, scrubbed farmhouse-type table in the centre of the room, and lots of gleaming modern equipment.

There were no answers to her dilemma here. She would have to dig deep inside herself for them, and she was afraid of what she might find. She couldn't betray Matthew without also betraying herself, and yet she couldn't walk away from Paul without him haunting her for the rest of her life. Wouldn't that be a betrayal in itself?

'Damn,' she muttered, biting her lip. 'Damn, damn, damn!'

'My sentiments entirely,' said an amused voice from the kitchen doorway.

Briony, slumped against one of the dressers, straightened up guiltily and looked towards the door. A woman several years older than herself stood there. She wasn't beautiful in the way Chantal was beautiful, but it didn't seem to matter because she had such tremendous style.

Her fair hair swept down in waves over her ears and rose to a gleaming chignon at the top of her head. Her make-up was bold, dramatically accentuating her pale skin and sapphire-blue eyes. Her lipstick was the precise shade of the pink trouser-suit she wore. It was beautifully cut from wild silk, screamed of *haute couture*, and shimmered as she strolled further into the kitchen.

Briony felt like a refugee from Oxfam as the woman surveyed her from top to toe with what seemed like studied insolence, and felt her hackles rising. This woman must be one of the latecomers she hadn't met. Once seen, she couldn't possibly be forgotten.

'Sheena Patterson,' she introduced herself.

'Briony Spenser.' The other woman hadn't extended her hand, so Briony didn't risk a snub by extending hers. She didn't know why, but she knew she was confronting an enemy.

She was proved right when Sheena said, 'So you're Paul's latest little diversion. I knew there had to be one when I wasn't invited to his party. My word, you did give yourself away when you were dancing with him! That was a terrible mistake, darling. Paul's a hunter—he tramples all over little girls who fall at his feet. It's a mistake I never make, which is why he always returns to me.'

She raised the glass she was carrying in her right hand and looked at Briony over the rim of it. She sipped slowly, then said, 'Just putting you in the picture, darling. Call it fellow feeling. After all, we are both women.'

Briony had never met anybody like her before and she didn't know how to cope. She fell back on the defensive, and said, 'You don't understand. I'm engaged to somebody else.'

'Ah!' Sheena breathed. 'That would make you irresistible, Paul being Paul. I knew there had to be a bit of spice somewhere. You're not at all his usual style. Now I know why he didn't invite me—he knew I'd laugh.'

Briony flushed and said heatedly, 'You've got it all wrong. This is Chantal's party, not Paul's.'

Sheena's delicate eyebrows rose. 'Chantal give a party before going away on a very important photographic assignment? If you believe that, you'll believe anything! She wouldn't risk the dark rings under her eyes. No, this is Paul's idea—to draw you into the trap, darling—and she went along with it. He has this most distressing ability to twist any female around his little finger.'

'Except you, of course,' Briony retaliated, annoyed enough to come off the defensive.

'Except me,' Sheena agreed sweetly. 'That's what gives me the edge with Paul and why he always comes back. My word, if looks could kill I'd be dead on the spot!' She smiled and began to drift towards the door. 'Hate me if you like, darling, but I'm only trying to put you wise. Listen, and you'll thank me one day. If you don't want to listen, that's up to you. It won't make the slightest difference to me and Paul in the long run.'

Briony couldn't think of a thing to say. Sheena's smile widened and she turned to a new target as Chantal came into the room. 'Naughty girl for not inviting me to the party,' she chided. 'You might have known I'd hear about it on the grapevine.'

She didn't wait for an answer but went back into the drawing-room. Chantal looked at Briony's flushed face and said, 'Sheena's been showing her claws, has she? I'm sorry. I wanted to warn you about her in case she turned up, but I didn't get the chance. She and Paul were a bit of an item at one time and she still regards him as her territory.'

'He certainly isn't mine,' Briony snapped, still seething.

'Are you very sure about that?' Chantal asked. 'I know you two have only just met, but sometimes that's all it takes.'

There it was again, that speculative look in the grey eyes that were so like Paul's. Briony looked away. 'He must have told you I'm engaged to somebody else,' she said.

'We all make mistakes.'

Briony didn't want to go into that. There were too many other things she needed to find out. 'Chantal, Paul told me at lunchtime you were having a going-away party, as if it was all arranged. Is that true?'

'No. He made it up because he couldn't think of any other way you'd agree to see him again.'

'Then the bit about bringing me along so you couldn't pair him off with somebody else was a lie as well,' Briony went on. 'Sheena was right—it was all a trap. I should be flattered he went to so much trouble, but I'm not. I trusted him. Sheena said he's only interested in me because I'm engaged to somebody else. That's rotten of him—and rotten of you to help him deceive me.'

'My word, Sheena has done her work well,' Chantal murmured. 'Don't you recognise spite when you hear it?'

'I recognise deceit. You didn't have to be a part of it.'

'But I did,' Chantal sighed. 'When Paul told me all about you, he was *different*. It's hard to explain, but I knew right away that you're special to him. If I'd thought for a moment you were just another girl I'd be curled up in bed now so I'll look my best tomorrow.'

She paused, looked at Briony's set face and waved a hand at the dishes of food on the table. 'Paul did all this. He made the cheese dip and rustled up the quiches and snacks from heaven knows where, considering it's a Sunday. He spent the entire afternoon on the go while I rested, and he made all the phone calls inviting people. He's never, ever, gone to so much trouble for any girl. He simply doesn't have to. Now if you were his sister, what would you have done?'

Briony was silent for a long while. Then she said, 'Given a party.'

Chantal's face broke into smiles. 'Oh, I do like you,' she said impulsively. 'I was worried I wouldn't, but when I saw you and Paul together I knew everything would be all right.'

'It couldn't be more wrong,' Briony protested. 'I'm engaged! I'm getting more and more muddled by the minute.'

'You poor thing, I do feel for you,' Chantal said, coming over and kissing Briony on the cheek again. 'I've been in a few predicaments myself. I can only advise you to concentrate on what's most important.'

'If only I knew what is,' Briony murmured wryly.

'I'd say it was discovering whether this feeling between you and Paul is a flash in the pan or not. You can hardly marry somebody else until you know.'

She made it sound so simple—too simple!—just as Paul had. Briony could only say, 'I love my fiancé.'

'It's possible to love a man for a lot of different reasons. It doesn't necessarily mean you're *in love* with him.' Chantal let the message sink in, then she put on oven gloves and went over to the cooker. 'If I don't rescue the jacket potatoes they'll be reduced to ashes. Would you be a honey and put the fillings on the serving trolley? The grated cheese, sweetcorn, coleslaw and prawns.'

Briony unwrapped the prepared dishes, but as she loaded them on to the trolley she said, 'Is this your way of telling me you've had enough of me and my problems?'

Chantal, her face prettily flushed from the cooker, threw her a quick look and grinned. 'No, it's my way of trying to be fair. You're the one who has to decide whether this feeling between you and Paul is worth pursuing.'

'Is it so obvious. . .this feeling?' Briony asked, catching her full lower lip between her teeth in anxiety.

'Very.' Chantal put a large dish of crisply baked potatoes on the trolley and began to fill another.

'What did you mean about being fair?'

'That I couldn't be. I don't know your fiancé, so I couldn't care less about him. I care very much about Paul, so I'll always be biased in his favour. We're very close, particularly since—well, never mind about that.'

'I mind very much,' Briony protested, laughing. 'There's nothing worse than being half told something!'

'All right—since David was killed in the Lebanon two years ago, reporting for the agency. He was our older brother. My fiancé Toby died with him. He was a photographer.'

The laughter drained from Briony's face. 'I'm so sorry,' she whispered. 'Trust me to put my foot in it!'

'No such thing!' Chantal denied. 'I didn't *have* to explain, but it's the only way you'll understand there isn't much I wouldn't do for Paul. Losing David was a terrible blow to the whole family. Losing Toby was——' She broke off, and when she spoke again it was quietly. 'I couldn't cope with that. I loved Toby so much I didn't want to live without him. I went to pieces. Paul put me back together again. He did what my parents were afraid to do in case they pushed me over the edge—he threw away the booze and tranquillisers and drove me back to work. He made me believe the real tragedy would have been if I'd never known Toby. It was a lifeline I could really hang on to.'

Briony was silent, unable to equate the lovely Chantal with so much suffering.

'There will never be another Toby,' Chantal continued, 'but enough time has passed now for me to hope to meet somebody else I can care about as much. If not—well, at least I've known what it's like to be truly happy, and that's more than some people can say.'

'And I thought you hadn't a care in the world,' Briony said wonderingly.

'Who hasn't a scar or two to hide?' Chantal asked, shrugging. 'I succeed so well because Toby lived life to the full, and that's what he'd have wanted me to do—something else Paul made me see.'

'It's the way he lives himself. I knew it immediately,' Briony replied, a certain wistfulness in her voice. 'For me, simply surviving is enough.'

'No, it's not, but Paul will teach you that.'

Briony shook her head. 'I just can't forget about Matthew—my fiancé.'

Chantal sighed. 'The way I understand it, you and Paul have a few days to sort that thorny problem out. Don't waste those days; you might never have any as precious again.'

Briony flushed slightly. 'I think you must be forgetting I'm just a girl he picked up in the street.'

'I'm not forgetting anything. In fact, it's the reason I'm sure you should hang on to each other, at least for the time being. Paul doesn't normally operate that way and I'm certain you don't either. Like it or not, you're important to each other.' Chantal laughed suddenly. 'Which brings me back to my original point. I'm all for making Paul happy. You'll just have to look after yourself.'

'Thanks very much. I like to know when I've met a friend,' Briony replied drily.

Chantal's eyes lit with approval. 'You'll do,' she said. 'Yes, I think you'll cope with Paul very nicely.'

Briony couldn't follow that up, because Paul came into the kitchen. Just the sight of him caused her heart to slip into that strangely erratic beat that left her breathless and excited. She realised with a flicker of dismay that if she had the same effect on him he hid it well. He looked from her face to Chantal's and said with his usual easy confidence, 'What's this, girlie talk? Whose character is being assassinated now?'

'Yours,' Chantal replied, her fine grey eyes sparkling with mischief. 'I've been telling Briony to run for the hills while she's still got the chance.'

Paul came over to Briony, raised her hand to his lips and kissed it. 'You won't do that, will you?' he asked intently. 'I'd only run after you.'

Briony's heart beat more erratically than ever, but after a lifetime of concealing her emotions she couldn't be as frank about them as Paul and Chantal were. She was lost for words and Chantal must have known it because she said, 'Paul, stop interfering with the kitchen staff or nobody will get fed. In fact, now you're here you can make yourself useful. Push this trolley through to the wolf pack. When you've unloaded it, come back for more.'

'Only if I can take Briony with me,' he bargained.

'Next time round,' Chantal promised, pushing the trolley in his direction.

'Slave-driver,' he grumbled, but he released Briony's hand and manoeuvred the trolley into the drawing-room.

When the door closed behind him, Briony expected his blatant flirting to raise some comment from Chantal, if only jokingly, but she said nothing. Perhaps she was too used to it to even notice. And that, Briony thought, should frighten me away from Paul where all else has failed. . .and yet she found it very difficult not to watch the door for his return. She didn't feel quite right without him close to her. It was almost as if a part of herself was missing.

Run for the hills, she mused, recollecting Chantal's joke. There wasn't much chance of that when she couldn't bring herself to run as far as the street! She was trapped here by her own crazily beating heart, unable to resist the excitement flooding her nervous system. It was almost like being drugged. Something pretty traumatic would have to happen to release her from the spell she was under.

Perhaps another talk with Sheena would do it. But, even as she thought of it, Briony knew it wouldn't happen. Chantal would see to that. She was, as she'd so freely confessed, strictly on Paul's side.

Well, Briony decided, temporarily abandoning the struggle for sanity, I can't say I haven't been warned!

Chantal lifted a stack of serving baskets from one

of the dressers and began tearing open packets of crisps and savoury biscuits to tip into them. 'To go with the cheese dip,' she explained, as Briony moved to help her. 'If anybody's still hungry after this lot they can come and raid the pantry themselves. I've had enough of the kitchen. I believe in enjoying my own parties.'

'Even if it's been thrust on you?' Briony asked. 'I've an awful feeling you'll be cursing Paul and me when you have to get up in the morning.'

'No fear of that,' Chantal assured her blithely. 'I'll get my beauty sleep. Paul made a point of warning everybody it's a Cinderella affair.'

Briony stopped shaking a large packet of pretzels into a basket and repeated in surprise, 'Cinderella affair? What's that?'

'Everybody has to vanish at midnight.'

'I should have guessed!' Briony's laughter softened as Paul came back into the room. The feeling that some part of her was missing vanished. She felt whole again, tinglingly alive with the most delicious sense of anticipation. Anticipation for what? It didn't matter. Paul was with her. . .

Once more she tried to remember whether Matthew had ever had this effect on her. If he had, surely she wouldn't have forgotten? They'd been apart months, not years. Such intensity of feeling must leave some mark, and yet all she was aware of was that Paul made her feel untouched, virginal.

He also made her feel wretched with guilt. Briony was unaware of the distressed frown drawing her dark, slanting eyebrows together, but Paul saw it. He abandoned the serving trolley, started to come towards her, then checked and went over to Chantal instead.

'Back to the party,' he said, putting an arm around her waist and urging her towards the door. 'I'm not giving you any chance to accuse me of being a slave-driver too.'

'Nonsense!' Chantal exclaimed, resisting. Then she saw something in his eyes that made her glance quickly from him to Briony. 'On the other hand, I was just saying I'd had enough of the kitchen,' she went on, and allowed herself to be pushed firmly from the room.

Paul came over to Briony. She was claustro-phobically aware of his closeness. Suddenly it was difficult to breathe, and she knew it was from the effort of constraining the excitement leaping like a wild thing within her. Paul lifted her face to his and massaged her eyebrows apart with strong but sensi-tive fingers. His touch was gentle, soothing, and Briony wanted to close her eyes and purr like a contented cat.

'No frowning allowed—house rules,' he said, his voice deep with a concern that was as seductive as his fingers.

Briony blinked her eyes open and tried to smile. It wasn't easy. She had never been so happy and yet so sad at one and the same time. She didn't know why she felt like this. . .no, that was a lie! She knew perfectly well why being with Paul alternately lifted her up and dragged her down. It was because she didn't have his ability to snatch what he wanted when he wanted it. She was hampered by a con-science, and how she wished she weren't!

Oh, Paul, she thought, whatever you're doing to me, please stop!

It was a cry from the heart, and it was to her shame that it was uttered in silence and lacked conviction. Paul was turning her into a creature of the flesh and, however much she hated herself, she was fascinated by how much the flesh could hunger. She had never known, never guessed. . .

'You're still frowning,' Paul reproved gently. 'I wish you wouldn't. It hurts me when you frown.'

Briony, looking deeply into his grey eyes, believed him. His concern cut right through her defences, weakening her when she most needed to be strong. She tried to mock herself, and him, by saying with a lightness she was far from feeling, 'You and your house rules! I bet you make them up as you go along.'

'Who doesn't?' he asked, smiling tenderly at her.

'I don't.' Briony tried hard to put some conviction into her denial. Frightened that she'd failed, she emphasised, 'I play it strictly by the book.'

'Forget the damned book, Briony!' Paul, his voice thickened with desire, seized her roughly by the shoulders and held her helpless. Before she could adjust to the sudden change, his lips came down savagely on hers.

# CHAPTER FIVE

PAUL's urgency communicated itself to Briony. She was emotionally as well as physically incapable of resisting him, and yet there was no joy in her surrender. He had already inflamed her senses and now he was inflaming her body and, whatever it was she wanted from him, her reeling mind knew it wasn't this.

It was too soon. She was too unsure, both of herself and him. While a passion she hadn't known she possessed flamed to match his, a tiny part of her mind remained detached. Paul seemed to sense it, and his searching lips became even more demanding. Too late, Briony tried to wrench her lips away, and found she had a battle on her hands.

Perhaps, if she'd had a real will to win, Paul would have let her go, but he also seemed to sense that her resistance was only token. One of his hands slid from her shoulders and found her breast. Briony gasped and the resistance drained from her. Her whole world seemed to shrink to that knowledge-able, massaging hand. Her nipples hardened and she arched her back, strained her breasts towards him in an attempt to ease the aching desire he aroused in her.

'Briony,' Paul murmured thickly. 'My lovely Briony. . .'

'Paul,' she gasped in a last attempt to regain sanity. 'Oh, Paul, please don't!'

'Not in the kitchen, at any rate. You might curdle the cheese dip,' said an amused voice Briony had already learned to loathe.

Her face flamed and she tried to push Paul away, but his grip on her took on the strength of steel. It didn't cross her mind that he was trying to shield her and she struggled even more wildly, but to no avail. She only wore herself out, and as she quietened in his arms he turned his face towards the door and said, 'Sheena, why don't you go and jump out of a window?'

'Because you'd only miss me tomorrow, or the day after, or however long it takes for this latest little adventure of yours to bore you to death,' Sheena replied, completely unruffled.

'Paul, please let me go,' Briony pleaded in an agony of embarrassment.

She'd only whispered, but Sheena heard her. 'Give him what he wants and he'll drop you like the proverbial hot brick,' she advised, smothering a well-simulated yawn.

'If you think that's funny. . .' Paul began angrily.

'Actually, darling, I find the whole situation pathetic. I think I'll leave you to it. I'll be in Paris for a few more days. You know where to find me when you want me, as you surely will, but Little Miss Innocent here doesn't know that, does she?'

A wave of her slender hand and she sauntered away, leaving behind her a heavy aroma of perfume—and malice. Briony was overwhelmed by both. She pushed Paul away and said unsteadily, 'I'm going too.'

He took hold of her shoulders again and replied, 'Briony, my love, if you'll just listen——'

'I am not your love!' she exclaimed, anger replacing her humiliation. Paul had stripped her emotions bare and, when she was at her most vulnerable, Sheena had mocked her. She could endure no more. All she wanted was to crawl away and hide herself until she could muster up some kind of dignity.

'You are very much my love,' Paul said steadily.

'So is everybody else, apparently,' she snapped.

His hands dropped from her shoulders. 'I suggest you leave the spite to Sheena. It's not your style.'

'You don't know my style, but I've got a pretty good idea what yours is!' Briony heard the shrill edge on her voice and hated it. She'd never sounded like this before, and never felt like it either—just a raw mass of quivering nerves. She fought hard for control and managed to say more calmly, 'Do I have to remind you of your promise to take me back to my hotel the minute I wanted to go?'

'You don't, but I'm not letting you leave like this.'

Briony eyed him warily. He was big, angry, and looked perfectly capable of doing anything he wanted. She shuddered with almost pleasurable fear, loathed herself for it, then realised there were enough people in the next room to guarantee her safety. 'You don't have a choice,' she told him coldly. 'I'm the one with the choices, and I choose to take myself home. Goodbye, Paul.'

'Now you're being silly,' he said.

'No!' she flared angrily. 'Now is when I *stop* being silly.'

She wished she could make a cool and graceful exit like Sheena, but it was with a decided flounce that she launched herself into the drawing-room. She pulled up short as she met a barrage of eyes. The music was turned low and everybody was sitting down eating. They were also all staring towards the kitchen. It was obvious they'd heard the quarrel.

Oh, lord, I want to die, she thought, but her spirit—wounded though it was—rallied to her support. She might not be as sophisticated as the Deverills and their friends, but at least she could show she wasn't wanting in manners. She went over to Chantal, extended her hand and said politely, 'Thank you for inviting me to your party. I do hope you enjoy your trip to the Bahamas.'

Chantal took her hand and held on to it. 'Do stay, if only to have something to eat,' she urged, looking over Briony's shoulder to Paul in silent appeal. It was the first clue Briony had that he'd followed her, and she felt distinctly uneasy.

'Quite a firecracker when she gets going, isn't she, my Briony?' Paul remarked in answer to his sister's silent enquiry.

*His* Briony! Where did he get the nerve! And this scene was supposed to be funny, was it? He was warped, he had to be. Matthew might not have his power to elate her, but he never made her feel so low either. And Matthew, bless him, never, ever laughed at her.

Briony had never wanted to hurt anybody before, but she could willingly have murdered Paul. It showed in her eyes as she turned her head to glower at him. 'More petals unfurling,' he said softly.

Briony stiffened, pulled her hand from Chantal's and stalked over to the lift. Somehow Paul got there before her and opened the door. She stepped in, glaring at him in a way that dared him to follow. Paul, though, was proof against such looks and crowded in with her. Briony retreated to the back of the lift, knowing there wasn't a thing she could do without an undignified and hopeless struggle.

She felt, as usual, overpowered by his closeness. She knew of no way to defend herself except, perhaps, by icy silence. He could hardly be proof against that.

'So you can sulk too,' Paul observed conversationally. 'I wish you'd tell me what I've done that is so dreadful.'

Briony ignored him.

'If I couldn't resist kissing you, you couldn't resist kissing me either,' he pointed out.

It was the last straw. How dared he be so reasonable about something that was anything but? Briony, who'd never struck anybody in her life before, raised her hand and slapped him hard across the cheek. He didn't attempt to avoid the blow. In fact, he took it so calmly she suspected he'd deliberately goaded her into it.

That didn't seem possible, but she knew she was right when he continued equably, 'I'm glad we've got that out of the way. If you feel better, perhaps we can talk—and you and I really need to talk.'

Briony was outraged rather than pacified. The lift stopped, and when Paul made no move to open the door she wrenched it back. She wanted to maintain a dignified silence, but her seething emotions wouldn't let her. 'I trusted you!' she burst out, fastidiously moving her shoulder to avoid contact with him as she stepped into the hall.

'You never trusted me,' Paul contradicted bluntly as he slammed the lift shut and followed her to the front door. 'If you had, Sheena could never have come between us.'

'There was nothing to come between, and how you of all people can talk of trust, I don't know! You've lied to me from the start.'

'Only because I had to see you again. Will it help if I promise to be truthful from now on?'

Paul's voice was deep. Briony looked up at him and was almost lost. How handsome he was, how sincere he sounded, and how easy it would be to capitulate. While his eyes held hers she wasn't even sure what they were fighting about. It was blurring already, like something that wasn't really important.

With a mammoth effort of will, Briony looked away. They were on the quay and quite alone. The lights were on all along the riverbank, turning this exclusive part of Paris into a shining wonderland. But the night air was cold and she shivered. In her impetuous departure she'd left her coat behind. It should have been a slipper, she thought in bitter self-mockery, as Chantal's words came back to her: 'it's a Cinderella affair'.

'Will it help?' Paul persisted.

Too soon, Briony's anger was draining from her, and her strength seemed to go with it. She felt weak and vulnerable and close to tears. 'It will help,' she replied, swallowing to relieve the ache in her throat, 'if you promise to leave me alone. That's all I want from you, Paul.'

'That's the one promise I can't make, and when you stop being so foolish you'll know it.' He opened the door of the sports car and added, 'Get in. You're shivering.'

He made Briony feel childish and petty. The ache in her throat became unbearable. There was so much she wanted to say, so much she had a right to say, but she couldn't speak. She got into the sports car like a lamb, cravenly avoiding another scene. If Paul was determined to take her home, nothing would change his mind. He seemed to thrive on opposition, whereas she—right now she was too close to breaking down and crying like a baby, and too fearful of crawling into his arms for comfort.

Paul began the drive back to her hotel. The streets were night-quiet, almost empty. He glanced at her. She averted her face and he said in exasperation, 'I know you're not very experienced, but surely even you can see that Sheena is a first-class bitch.'

Briony's flagging spirit revived like magic at what she suspected was ridicule. She snapped, 'She speaks highly of you as well. She thinks you're a first-class bastard. Me, I think you're both right!'

There was a stunned silence, then Paul began to laugh. 'Ah, Briony, how could I help but fall for you?' he asked caressingly. 'All these new petals unfurling, and each so different. I never know what you're going to say next. You should pity me, not blame me, for finding you irresistible.'

'Pity you!' she exclaimed, incensed. 'I wouldn't dare. You'd only take advantage of me.'

'How well you're getting to know me,' he murmured.

His amusement struck no answering chord in Briony and she muttered something not very nice under her breath. Paul laughed again and said, 'That does it. Matthew will have to find himself another woman. You're definitely mine.'

'Stop it!' she said. 'Just stop it! I don't share your warped sense of humour. Tonight was an experiment that didn't work out, and that's the end of it.'

'You talk a lot of nonsense, my darling.'

*His darling*! For a treacherous moment Briony wished she were, then better sense prevailed. 'If you think that, it's because you have no values—and no morals either!' she retorted.

'I'm a sad case,' Paul agreed. 'I need you to save me from myself. Come on, now, Briony, what woman could resist a challenge like that?'

'Try Sheena,' she suggested.

'I did, and it didn't work out,' he replied brazenly. 'Let me tell you about Sheena——'

'Thanks, but I don't want to know,' Briony interrupted. 'It's none of my business.'

'All right.' Paul dropped his banter and went on seriously, 'We'll stick to what is your business. You came to Paris to find out who you really are, and I'm a part of it now.'

'No!' she denied.

'Yes,' he went on inexorably. 'For safety's sake you're trying to hang on to the girl you used to be—Matthew's girl. But she's gone, my little love, and she won't come back. You need to live and laugh and truly love, and you can't do that without risking yourself a little. Deep down you know it, and that's why you're so mad at me. It's got nothing to do with Sheena or Matthew, it's all to do with us.'

He paused and glanced at her. When she said nothing, he went on, 'I told you when we met it was a beginning. We're nowhere near the middle and, if we're lucky, we'll never reach the end. What we have is a once-in-a-lifetime thing, and I know it if you don't.'

Briony was devastated by his words. They rang so true, and yet she knew what he didn't, that she couldn't let Matthew go. It wasn't something she could explain, only feel. She and Matthew had already shared so much, while she and Paul. . .

'It's my lifetime as well as yours,' Paul continued determinedly, 'and what's mine I hang on to.'

She bowed her head, scarcely noticing they had reached her hotel until Paul parked. He turned towards her and touched her averted cheek with lightly caressing fingers. 'Poor little darling,' he said softly. 'I know it's too much for you to take just now, but I'll teach you to trust me. I'll pick you up at ten tomorrow and we'll talk about all the things we never got around to tonight. You'd better go now or I'll be kissing you again, and I try never to make the same mistake twice in one evening.'

Briony didn't argue. For the second time that evening, she fled from him.

The night brought no counsel and no wisdom. She breakfasted early on a crusty roll and coffee and miserably decided there was only one way out for her, and that was to avoid Paul altogether. No man liked to be stood up, even by a girl who hadn't agreed to a date, and all it would take would be a little resolution on her part.

It took a whole lot more than that, but at nine o'clock, a whole hour before Paul was due, she crept down the stairs like a fugitive from her own longings and handed her key in at the reception desk.

As she turned towards the doors, a tall and handsome man rose from one of the deep armchairs in the reception area. 'Paul. . .' she whispered, the flush rising to her pale cheeks betraying the sudden pumping of her heart.

'Who else?' he asked, the smile she thought she would never see again playing havoc with her defences.

'You said ten o'clock,' she accused.

'Yes, but we both know what a devious character I am.' His fingers touched her cheek in the light caress that had haunted her dreams and made her reach out blindly for him so many times. 'Sleep well, my little love?' he asked.

'Paul, please! I am not your little love,' Briony said brokenly.

'You are, but I'll try to slow down to your pace. It won't be easy—we only have five days. Let's not waste any of them.' He took her hand and led her out into the street. Yesterday's rain had vanished as though it had never been. They stood there in the sunshine and stared at each other.

Paul said, 'I thought the Eiffel Tower and then a cruise on the Seine if this weather holds.'

'I shouldn't,' Briony said. 'I really shouldn't.'

The morning rush was on. Oblivious to the people hurrying around them, Paul cupped her face in his hands. He read the worry in her eyes and his face softened. 'Today we'll just be tourists,' he promised. 'You can't object to that. Besides, you'll never get your raincoat back unless you come with me. It's in the car.'

Still Briony hesitated. 'Just tourists?' she repeated, wanting to be absolutely positive there was no misunderstanding between them.

'Just tourists,' he reaffirmed, adding with a grin, 'You can always slap me again if I step out of line.'

He was so impossible, she had to laugh, and as she stepped into the sports car she knew the magical power he had to make her feel carefree and irresponsible was working again.

Being Paul, he cheated almost from the start. When they arrived at the Eiffel Tower and stepped into the lift, he held her hand. 'That's not just being tourists,' she objected.

'No, it's in case you get scared. It's a long way up.'

'Heights don't bother me.'

'You're not at the top yet,' he said. 'Besides, holding your hand is just being friendly. It's when I kiss it—like this—that it becomes something more. Stop shaking your head at me. That was simply a demonstration so you'd know the difference.'

He was as outrageous as he was impossible, but Briony found it even more impossible not to respond to him. When they left the lift and walked over to the barrier to look down on the vast sprawl of the city, it was more than the altitude that had gone to her head.

Paul pointed out the various landmarks, but it was her face he was watching, and it was his face she really wanted to look at. He was still holding her hand and, linked like this, she was conscious of a closeness that was more than physical. He kissed her hand again. She didn't object, because she understood.

He didn't press his luck but turned from her, pointed out another landmark and began to talk about it. Briony was grateful. It showed he was beginning to understand her too.

When they came down from the tower, the sun was taking on real summer-like heat. Paul bought ice-creams and they strolled hand in hand among the close-mown lawns while they were eating them. Briony looked at the flower-beds, a blaze of purple and yellow, and said, 'The pansies are pretty. I love pansies. I've got them in my window-box at home.'

'No garden?' Paul asked.

'Hardly!' she chuckled. 'I share my quarters in the hotel with another receptionist, and it isn't exactly a room with a view, unless you count the dustbins. Still, I'll have a garden one day. It won't be neat and formal like this. It will be Old English to attract the butterflies and bees, with masses of hollyhocks and other flowers that have gone out of fashion.'

'Bees don't bother you?'

Briony shook her head. 'I like to listen to them. They make a happy sound—busy, but happy. Once I was fostered out with a couple who had a garden like that. I wanted so much to stay, but they only did short-term fostering. Still, it was nice while it lasted.'

She didn't realise how wistful she'd become, but Paul did. His hand tightened momentarily on hers, and he replied, 'You'd get on well with my mother. Part of her garden runs riot with flowers, and she never uses insecticide. She says it's better to let the good bugs fight the bad bugs.'

'She's right, and she sounds nice,' Briony responded impulsively.

'She is. Would you like to meet her?'

She was taken aback. When she recovered, she asked, 'Is she coming to Paris?'

'No, but we could soon fly to England.'

'Good heavens, no!' she exclaimed. 'She'd think there was something between us.'

'Isn't there?'

Briony looked away, unable to answer. Paul realised he had gone too far. He didn't give up, just switched his angle slightly. 'Of course, I couldn't guarantee butterflies and bees at the beginning of March, but something's bound to be flowering. It always is, and spring comes as early to Dorset, where my parents live, as it does to any part of England. We could stay for a night or two, or just make it a day trip.'

Briony was deeply tempted, but she shook her head, afraid of the implications. Paul, after a fractional hesitation, didn't make an issue of it. He began to talk of something else, and she warmed towards him. Once more he was showing a tact she hadn't credited him with.

Or was the hunter becoming cunning?

The thought came unbidden into her mind and she brushed it aside, knowing it had been planted there by the spiteful Sheena. Besides, it was totally at odds with the way she was feeling. She had been scorched by the flames of passion in Paul's arms, but this warmth suffusing her entire being was entirely different.

He wanted to take her to his parents' home, and she couldn't think of a greater compliment. Nor was it the sort of behaviour likely from the predatory hunter poised for the kill that Sheena had described.

It was possible, of course, that Paul was two people—just as she had become since she'd met him—only with him it was permanent. It was a disquieting thought, and she looked up at him anxiously. He smiled at her and the anxiety faded. They were just tourists, after all.

# CHAPTER SIX

PAUL drove Briony south to visit Napoleon's Tomb, an experience that left her speechless. When they came out again into the sunshine, she murmured, 'I've never seen anything like it. It's all a bit over the top, isn't it?'

He smiled. 'Well, there's no missing Nelson on top of his column in Trafalgar Square.'

'Perhaps not, but I don't even know where Wellington's buried, and he beat Napoleon at Waterloo.'

'With the help of the Prussians.'

Briony pulled a face at him. 'Do you fly your Union Jack at half-mast?'

'No, but I did warn you I have a foot in both camps. I'll whistle a few bars of "Rule Britannia" if it will make you feel any better.'

She chuckled. 'You think I'm absurd, don't you?'

'No, I think you're delightful and a lot of other things besides—but you'll only think I'm flirting with you if I start going into them. Where do you want to go next? The military museum? It's almost lunch-time, but we could manage a few of the galleries.'

Briony shook her head. 'I've had enough of military glory for one day. After all that gloomy marble, I need a stiff drink.'

Paul laughed. 'Spoken like a girl after my own heart—if you hadn't already stolen it!'

She pulled a face at him, thinking he was teasing her, but the warmth within her took on a new glow. She loved this talent he had for making her feel special, even if she didn't entirely believe in it.

He took her to a restaurant designed like a ship where they lunched on fish soup and grilled salmon. He ordered champagne again, although she demurred, 'You shouldn't. It isn't necessary.' Thinking about how she'd slept away yesterday afternoon, she added, 'Besides, I think champagne makes me sleepy.'

'Don't put ideas into my head!'

Briony looked at him over the rim of her glass and scolded, 'You never miss a trick, do you?'

'Don't give up on me. I'm trying to mend my evil ways. I just need a little more of your excellent tuition.'

She choked on her champagne, laughter as bubbly as the wine at his outrageousness rising within her. Oh, he was such fun! The danger was in taking him seriously, but she wasn't fool enough to take him seriously. Or so she thought until she found herself asking the question she'd been determined *not* to ask. 'Who is Sheena?'

'I was hoping you'd mention her.'

Briony was sorry she had, but she had to bluff it through, and she hoped her 'Why?' was casual enough.

Paul's hand came across the table and covered hers. 'She's an unnecessary barrier between us.'

She had to resist the impulse to turn her hand to clasp his. It seemed so natural, somehow. Afraid she'd started something she couldn't see the end of, she said lightly, 'As a barrier, she's nothing compared to Matthew. I was just curious, that's all.'

He withdrew his hand. Did he realise he'd touched her long enough for her to miss the contact? All she knew was that she wished he were touching her still. What was wrong with her, for heaven's sake? She couldn't go on reacting this positively to his slightest contact!

Paul, though, seemed to have withdrawn into a world of his own. After a while, he said, 'Chantal and I had a long talk last night. I gather she told you about my brother's death.'

'Yes, and Toby's. I'm so sorry.'

He nodded, then went on, 'She didn't tell you about all the repercussions, not as they affected me, anyway. My father was set to retire completely, and David was being groomed to step into his shoes. With him gone, there's only me, and I'm not ready for a desk job yet. My family thinks if I marry and settle down, I will be. They also think Sheena is the one to do it.'

'I see,' Briony replied, a pain in her heart that surprised her by its intensity. Paul and Sheena—two sophisticated, self-confident people. A natural match.

'You don't,' Paul contradicted. 'Sheena has her fascination, I won't lie about that. We had an on-off affair for years, but it was never going anywhere. I never felt the least urge to marry her, nor did she want to marry me until David's death put me in the number one position to take over the agency. She's a very ambitious woman.'

'Is that bad?' Briony asked, the pain in her heart easing.

'She can be any sort of a woman she likes, but she'll never be my woman. That certain something is missing.'

Briony felt a little dazed, remembering his telling her that she was his woman. She remembered other things as well, and didn't know what to make of it all. There seemed an incredible amount of things to remember about Paul, and yet she'd known him only twenty-four hours. Surely it was only a poetic thing that sometimes it was possible to know all there was to know about a person in a single glance. It couldn't possibly be real.

But when had anything to do with Paul ever been real?

'What does Sheena do?' she asked, needing to know more about the woman he frankly described as fascinating.

'She's a freelance journalist, a top-notch one. She specialises in features for international news magazines. Sometimes she supplies stuff to us.'

'Then it's understandable why your family thinks she's right for you,' Briony replied, thinking that a budding hotel manager who hadn't got past a receptionist's desk was hardly in the same league.

'I'm not looking for a business arrangement,' Paul replied bluntly. 'If I thought she was essential for the agency, I'd hire her, not marry her. When I marry it will be to a girl I can't live without, and to hell with the agency.'

Briony's pulses fluttered. How exciting it would be to be loved in such a way! Paul never did anything by halves. She went weak at the knees at the thought of being essential to such a man.

'Would you marry for any reason but love?' he asked.

'No.'

'That's what I'm banking on,' he replied, and smiled at her in a way that sent her pulses haywire.

She began to wonder whether he was deliberately keeping her in a turmoil to stop her from thinking straight. After all, she had both his and Sheena's version of their relationship, and no way of knowing which was speaking the truth. Paul could be as deceitful as Sheena was spiteful.

She had only her instincts to go on, and how reliable were they when she melted physically every time Paul touched her? She needed Sheena's ability to stand back from the situation and mock, but it was an ability she didn't have.

'Briony, promise me you'll never marry for anything but love.'

'I thought I just did.'

'It wasn't a promise,' he said.

She smiled and said lightly, 'Oh, I could promise anybody that.'

'I'm not anybody. Promise *me*.'

His fierceness stunned her. 'I promise,' she heard herself saying, and knew it was a vow.

Paul relaxed. 'Thank you. For the moment that's all I need to know.'

Briony was thrilled and bewildered by the intensity of emotion that could flare between them. To cool the situation, she said after a pause, 'Your father must be disappointed you're not ready for management. I mean, if he wants to retire for good.'

'He changed his mind when David died, although only temporarily. Work was the best therapy to come to terms with what happened.'

'For Chantal too,' Briony mused, thinking of what his sister had said.

'For all of us. I'm not being pressured at the moment, but I know the sooner I settle down, the happier they'll be. And,' he added, raising his glass in a silent toast to her, 'I'm beginning to think I'll be happier too.'

Once more Briony didn't know what to say. His implication was clear, and her heart began to thump in what was becoming an all too familiar painful way. She felt the betraying flush rise to her cheeks and bent her head.

Paul studied her for a moment, and apparently took pity on her. His manner changed and he continued briskly, 'I was forgetting—today we're just tourists. Where would you like to go next?'

'Paul,' she said impulsively, 'it must be a bore taking me to places you've already seen before. You really don't have to——'

'The delightful thing about you, Briony,' he broke in, 'is that you never bore me. What is more delightful is that I know you never will. Why do you think I'm hanging on to you so grimly? In a very wide experience, believe me, you're unique.'

She blushed more fiercely than ever. 'I wish you wouldn't talk like that.'

'All right, I won't, but it's very difficult when I've promised to be truthful. What do you think about making the most of this weather while it lasts and taking a trip along the Seine?'

Briony would have agreed to anything that took the pressure off her, but it was with real pleasure that she nodded. 'I'd like that.'

They returned to the riverbank by the Eiffel Tower just as a boat was about to depart. Laughing, they ran on board. 'It's a pity all the front seats are taken,' Briony said, as Paul led her to seats in the middle of the boat.

'Wait,' he replied, and to her delight the glass roof slid back as the cruise began.

The people at the front moved back to sit in the open sunshine, and she murmured, 'You've done this before.' With Sheena? she wondered, but that was a question that couldn't be asked. She had no right to sound jealous, even if she was.

It was only the beginning of March, but the sun was so hot it might have been high summer. She stripped off her sweater. Underneath she had a white T-shirt, but she regretted wearing her jeans. They were practical for sightseeing, but a skirt would have been cooler. Paul, in lightweight tan trousers and a tan cotton shirt, had judged the weather better. He'd rolled up the sleeves of his shirt and unbuttoned the collar, and he looked so manly she found it hard to pay attention to what the multi-lingual guide was saying over the microphone.

She was more preoccupied with the fact that Paul seemed to have lost interest in holding her hand. Exasperated with herself, she said as an island came into view, 'Is that where you live?'

'No, the next island along. This is the Ile de la

Cité. All that greenery at the tip is known as the Garden of the Green Lover—the Square du Vert-Galant—after a French king who supposedly had fifty-six mistresses.'

'A man after your own heart?' she asked.

'Not since I met you.'

Briony wished she'd held her tongue. Paul was using again the gift he had for making her feel so special. The trouble was she didn't know how much he spread the gift around. An image of the uncomplicated Matthew shot into her mind and, with it, guilt.

Once she had got over the novelty of being with someone like Paul, she'd been expecting Matthew to eclipse him completely, but the reverse was happening. Paul was eclipsing Matthew. It couldn't last, she reassured herself, it really couldn't last.

It seemed strange that Paul should take her hand just then, as though he sensed she was mentally slipping away from him. Yet that was the way it seemed and, wraith-like, Matthew's image faded from her mind. He simply couldn't survive the impact that physical contact with Paul had on her senses.

She found herself thinking of Paul's hungry lips and hands when he'd kissed her last night, and her equally hungry response. A warmth that had nothing to do with the sun glowed through her, and she pulled her T-shirt away from her neck in an unconscious cooling gesture.

'Are you all right?' asked Paul.

'I'm fine. I was just thinking. . .' Oh, no, she couldn't tell him what she'd just been thinking!

'Yes?' he prompted.

'I was just thinking how. . .how funny it is, Chantal flying off to the sunshine when we've got so much here.' Briony knew she was babbling, but anything to get away from the embarrassment she'd brought on herself by remembering things better forgotten. 'Did she get away all right?'

'Not a single hitch.'

She bit her full lower lip. 'I should have asked before, but it was a bit awkward, considering the way I left the party.'

'She understood. Do you always bite your lip when you feel awkward? You make me want to kiss it better.'

She looked quickly at him. 'Don't you dare!'

'Of course not,' said Paul, and kissed her swiftly and softly on the lips.

Briony's heart fluttered. She knew she should scold him, but the words wouldn't come. He made life such fun, and she was weary of always being serious. Would it be so terribly hard, or so terribly wicked, to learn how to flirt as lightly and amusingly as he did?

'Don't look so worried,' he whispered, his breath on her ear making her want to nuzzle her head against his. 'I'm not going to sail off into the sunset with you. There are too many people on the boat.'

That made her laugh, and when she could she said, 'I wouldn't put it past you.'

'Don't dare me. As you've just found out, I can never resist a dare.'

'So that's the reason you kissed me,' she replied

demurely, looking at him from under her long eyelashes.

'That's the reason I had ready in case you slapped me—and one more look like that and I'll be kissing you again!'

Briony blushed and looked so adorably confused that he released her hand and put his arm around her shoulders. She didn't resist. She was too busy thinking that it wasn't so terribly hard to flirt, after all. Whether or not it was wicked she would worry about some other time. As Paul had pointed out, she would never test the strength of her attachment to Matthew without risking herself a little. She needed someone to compare him with.

'Penny for them,' Paul offered. When she didn't answer immediately, he asked, 'Do I have to raise the bidding?'

'I was thinking Paris is nicer than my first impression of it.'

'Fibber! That's not really what you were thinking at all.'

'No,' she admitted, 'but that's all you're getting from me.'

He laughed. 'You're learning, Briony! All right, then, we'll talk about Paris. Most people fall in love with it straight away. I gather you didn't?'

'Far from it. It was all too much of a muchness for me—all those arrow-straight boulevards flanked with the same flat-fronted buildings of seven or eight storeys, and all leading to star-shaped intersections. It struck me as too uniform and organised, like an architect's city that wasn't really meant for people. It's not muddled and human and cosy like London, is it? I'm country-reared and I never thought I'd miss London, but I did on my first day here. London still has its funny nooks and crannies and greens to show it's grown out of a lot of villages. Paris looks as though it was created for effect. Now I'm on the river I can see its charm, but I couldn't before.'

Briony was surprised at her own garrulity, and a little abashed. Normally she kept her opinions to herself for fear of ridicule, and here she was sounding off to Paul about a city he loved. She waited for him to shoot her down in flames, and serve her right, for her first impression of Paris had been warped by her own misery.

'I suppose that's me for the guillotine,' she mumbled.

He smiled. 'Give me time, and I'll convert you. You made two mistakes in coming to Paris for the first time. You came at the beginning of March instead of the beginning of April, when all the trees are in bloom. Paris looks beautiful in the spring, but the sun's shining today, so perhaps that will help to make up for it.'

'And the second mistake?' she asked.

'You came alone. Any strange city can be depressing on your own, but that's remedied now. That's why you're beginning to see Paris in a different way.'

'You mean it isn't just the river?'

'I hope not,' Paul replied, tightening his arm around her shoulders.

She turned her face towards him and wished she hadn't, because his was so very close. 'You still don't miss a trick, do you?' she replied indignantly.

'I'm not playing for tricks. I'm playing for keeps.'

His seriousness alarmed her and her shoulders stiffened. He loosened his arm a trifle and went on much more lightly, 'If it's funny nooks and crannies you want, I'll take you to Montmartre. You won't be able to complain about anything being arrow-straight and organised there. Paris, like London, has its different faces if you know where to look for them.'

They had coffee when they got off the boat, then, as they strolled towards the car, a street photographer snapped them. 'Take two,' Paul said, and as they posed he explained to Briony, 'That's one for each of us. We should both have something to remember today with.'

Briony didn't think she'd ever forget, but Paul had so many more memories to keep in order than she had. By this time next year he might not even remember the colour of her eyes—or, worse, her name. A tiny shudder of future sadness touched her, almost a premonition, but she shrugged it away. Heavens, it wasn't as if she was the least bit psychic!

Paul was holding out both photographs to her. 'You choose,' he said.

She studied them. The first snap had been taken while they were walking along, and they were both smiling. They looked happy. The second had been posed. Paul had pulled her against his shoulder and, as she'd nestled there, he'd bent his head to kiss her hair. She hadn't known about that, but there it was, a romantic moment frozen for all time.

Briony desperately wanted the romantic snap, but she was afraid to say so. Paul might guess. . .guess what? Everything she was trying to hide from herself? 'I'll have this one,' she said, taking the first snap.

'A shrewd choice,' he said, putting the romantic photograph in his shirt pocket. 'It wouldn't do for Matthew to see this one, would it?'

It wouldn't do for Matthew to see either, she thought, although she'd never known him to show jealousy. Not that she'd ever given him cause. She put her photograph in her shoulder-bag, knowing she'd have to tear it up when she returned to London. Matthew might not understand that in Paris she'd become a different person for a little while. He might not even understand why she'd come to Paris at all. She wasn't so sure herself any more.

'Have you thought of him today?' asked Paul.

'Several times,' she lied, knowing it wasn't that often.

'I must be slipping!'

Briony laughed, but he shook his head in mock sorrow. 'It isn't funny. I'll have to try harder tomorrow.'

Tomorrow, she thought. Three more tomorrows after that, and then no more Paul. She shivered again, and this time he noticed. 'What's the matter? You can't be cold in this heat.'

'Nothing's the matter. A ghost walked over my grave, that's all.'

'It was probably mine—making sure you don't run away while I'm not looking.'

'I won't run away,' she said, forgetting to be guarded.

'That, Briony,' Paul replied, putting his arm

around her shoulders and hugging her against him, 'is the nicest thing you've said all day.'

She disentangled herself, feeling a little breathless. Afraid she'd given too much away, she retorted, 'I was about to say you're much too useful as a chauffeur.'

'Yes, ma'am!' Paul saluted her smartly. 'Do you want me to wear a cap tomorrow, or will nothing less than a complete uniform satisfy you?'

Briony pretended to consider carefully, then she said, 'I'll excuse you from the full uniform. I didn't pack my furs, you see. I'm travelling very informally.'

'How would you like to travel over my shoulder in a fireman's lift?'

She shook her head mournfully. 'I knew you were a bully the first time I met you.'

'After all I've done to hide it too!'

Briony laughed. Somewhere in the middle of her laughter it dawned on her how fatally easy it would be to mistake where the laughter ended and the love began. . .

# CHAPTER SEVEN

BRIONY was delighted with Montmartre. The little shops and houses were all jumbled up and it was teeming with people. She dragged Paul into an open-fronted shop and raked through a huge pile of colourful T-shirts, unable to resist the market atmosphere.

'Only two-fifty!' she exclaimed, doing a quick bit of currency translation. 'And just as I was beginning to think I could never afford anything in Paris. I was obviously shopping in the wrong area.' She pulled out a cotton T-shirt that was a chequer-board of pink and black squares and held it against her. 'Oh, yes, this will do nicely. I'll be desperate for something light to wear if this hot weather keeps up. I packed mostly heavy sweaters.'

Paul looked at the T-shirt and said, 'I saw a blouse in Galeries Lafayette the other day that was just made for you. Why don't you let me buy it for you?'

Briony was stung and all her pleasure evaporated. So this T-shirt was too cheap for somebody he was escorting around Paris, was it? On her first afternoon here she'd visited the fashionable Galeries Lafayette. True, she'd yearned for just about everything she'd seen, but she hadn't been able to afford to buy.

'It was pink silk,' he went on. 'It would look marvellous on you.'

'No, thanks, she snapped. 'Not even Matthew buys my clothes.' He'd never been able to afford it, but that was beside the point.

Unprepared for her sudden change of mood, Paul retorted, 'Don't be so proud. Buying it would mean nothing to me.'

'Buy it for Sheena, then. I suppose she was with you at the time.'

Her temper ignited his and he snapped back, 'If you must know, it was Chantal—and I'm damned if I know what the devil you're making such a fuss about!'

'That's probably because you're used to buying clothes for your women, but I am *not* one of your women!'

'You don't have to tell me that,' Paul said bitterly. 'None of my women would behave the way you're behaving.'

'Thank you, that's the nicest compliment you've paid me all day!' she flashed, flinging his own words back at him.

They were glaring at each other, and people in the crowded shop were turning to stare. For once, Briony couldn't have cared less. Something Chantal had said last night was ringing in her ears: 'it's a Cinderella affair'. She had been describing the party but, Briony thought furiously, she could just as easily have been describing me and Paul.

And I am not Cinderella!

Head high, she stalked away from Paul to the cash desk. Unfortunately, there was a queue and she had to wait. She stuck it out because by now she would have bought the T-shirt even if she'd hated it. Her temper was waning, but she told herself it was more than a storm in a teacup, it was the principle of the thing.

Paul came over and stood beside her. He dropped a kiss on her hair. 'Sorry. It was very insensitive of me to offer you a silk blouse from Galeries Lafayette. I just wanted you to have it. I simply didn't think.'

Briony looked up at him and what she saw in his eyes killed the last of her anger. 'I'm sorry too. I didn't mean to get so mad,' she said huskily.

'Fainites, then?'

A smile quivered to her lips. 'When I was a child we used to say "fainites and feet off ground" when we wanted a truce.'

'You must have been a lovely child.' Paul's voice deepened as he went on, 'We have so much to catch up on about each other, and so little time to do it in. Don't let's waste any of it quarrelling.'

His urgency struck an answering chord in her. She wanted to put her head against his chest, close her eyes and agree with him. She almost did, but it was her turn for service, and by the time she'd bought the T-shirt the weakness had passed. Or almost.

They were very polite and very careful with each other for a few minutes, and then they fell back into their old easy camaraderie. They went into a lot more shops, but Briony didn't buy anything, and as they walked up the approach road to the massive hill crowned by the Sacré-Coeur, Paul looked at Briony's reflective expression and asked, 'What are you thinking about now?'

'I'm trying to think what part of London Montmartre reminds me of.'

'Don't. It's uniquely French.'

'I could hum a few bars of the "Marseillaise" if you like,' she offered demurely.

Paul burst into laughter, then gave her another of his quick hugs. 'You little witch!' he breathed.

'What a lot of little things I am,' she retorted. 'Little love. . .little witch. . .'

'Little flirt,' he supplied.

The animation fled from her face and she said swiftly, 'I didn't mean to be. Honestly I didn't.'

'That's Matthew's girl speaking, and today I'm trying to kid myself you're mine. You're much more fun when you're mine, Briony.'

'This isn't the real me,' she insisted vehemently. 'Nobody's ever their real selves on holiday.'

'Have it your own way. I'm not going to quarrel with you any more today.' Paul came to a stop, and Briony with him, as they came into the open at the base of the steep climb to the white basilica at the top of the hill. The heat of the sun really hit them.

'It's beautiful,' she breathed, 'but it's going to be a hot climb up all those steps.'

'We'll take the funicular up and walk down,' he decided. 'There's a café at the top where we can have some tea before we go into the church.'

They did as he suggested, and when the cable-car trundled them up to the top and they'd refreshed themselves at the café they went into the Sacré-Coeur. Briony bought and lit a candle, she wasn't sure what for. She wasn't a Catholic or even particularly religious, but the atmosphere got to her.

All she could be certain of was that she was responding to a need for guidance. She felt one sort of love for Matthew and another for Paul—she couldn't deny that even to herself any more—and what the end of it all would be she couldn't begin to guess.

'Do you want to go up into the dome?' Paul whispered in her ear.

'I wouldn't miss it for the world,' she whispered back, trying to bring herself back to normality. 'Who knows when I'll be in Paris again?'

She was trying to be flippant, but she knew that while Paul was in Paris she wouldn't ever want to leave. It was fortunate they were both due to depart on the same day. She looked back at her candle as he led her away. It was burning brightly, but its flame had only a limited time to run.

Like me and Paul, she thought, and was seared with a pain suspiciously like heartbreak.

'Do you want to see the vaults as well?' he asked.

'In for a penny. . .' she began with a laugh that didn't ring true to her own ears. She was a tourist, she had to behave like one.

Paul bought tickets and they went down into the massive stone crypt first. It was impressively built, but it was cold, and after they'd looked at a few tombs Briony shivered. She'd left her sweater in the car.

'Let's get you back into the sunshine,' Paul said, and they began the long winding climb to the dome. Just as she was beginning to think the stone steps would never end they came out into the sunshine. She was breathless.

Paul opened his arms and she fell into them, collapsing against his chest while she waited for her breathing to even out. His arms closed around her and she closed her eyes, her head snuggling into his shoulder. She could feel the warmth of his body, the hardness of his muscles, and her breathing became ragged again. Feeling she had to say something to account for hanging on to him, she raised her head finally and managed, 'It's hard work being a tourist.'

He didn't answer. He looked down at her upturned face and her lips parted as she saw the expression in his eyes. Slowly his lips came down to cover hers and she surrendered without a struggle to the emotion uniting them. In a curious way it was a kiss without passion, almost as if each of them was recognising what was their own.

When they parted, both were shaken. 'I didn't mean to do that,' Paul said unsteadily.

'I know.' Briony turned from him and looked down over Paris. It was a closer, more intimate view than it had been from the Eiffel Tower.

'You're not mad at me?' he asked.

She shook her head, a deep awareness within her knowing that the time for anger had passed.

'You know I'm in love with you,' he said.

Again she shook her head. 'No, I don't know that.'

'What you mean is that you won't admit you're in love with me,' he replied, the roughness in his voice reacting abrasively on her own raw emotions.

'No, I don't mean that either,' she sighed. She turned from the panoramic view to look at him, determined to make him understand. 'What I mean is, I'm not sure of anything. I need time. . .'

'The one thing we haven't got!'

'Four more days,' she whispered. 'I need those days. Please don't hold a gun at my head. Matthew isn't the sort of man I can ditch overnight. I'd never forgive myself. . .'

Her voice trailed away because she knew that if Paul kissed her again, if he demanded the response she was incapable of refusing, her old loyalties and values would vanish as though they had never been. But they would return and they would spoil whatever she and Paul had, if they had anything.

Paul, though, lived for today, so how could he possibly understand? To try to make him, she went on, 'If—if—we still feel. . .the way we're feeling now. . .at the end of the week, I'll stop fighting. I just can't be engaged to one man and—and. . .' She broke off, floundering helplessly. All she could add was, 'It wouldn't be fair.'

She knew she'd made a mess of explaining her feelings, so she could only look at him appealingly, her brown eyes wide and vulnerable. Paul looked into them for endless moments, then smiled crookedly at her. 'All right, Briony, four more days of just being tourists, then we'll see.'

'Thank you,' she breathed, and felt so relieved she hugged him.

This time it was Paul who disentangled himself. He said wryly, 'I don't want your gratitude. Apart from that, you can hug me any time you like.'

She smiled, as he meant her to, and after that it seemed natural to hold hands as they walked around the outside of the dome. 'Seen enough?' he asked finally. She nodded, and he continued, 'I'll take you back to your hotel and pick you up at eight for dinner.'

'You don't have to——' she began.

'Yes, I do,' he broke in. 'I'm not letting you run around Paris by yourself.'

'There's a perfectly good restaurant just across the road from my hotel. You don't have to spend all your time with me,' she protested, finally managing to finish her sentence.

With a lazy finger Paul traced the line of her cheekbone, then brushed his finger across her lips. It was the lightest of touches, and yet so sensual. Involuntarily her lips parted and she caught his finger between her teeth. They looked at each other and then both stepped apart.

'I was going to say I *do* have to spend all my time with you,' said Paul. 'Don't you want to be with me?'

Briony looked down at her feet without answering. He studied her bowed head and asked, 'Do I take it that means yes?'

Silently she nodded, and when she finally raised her eyes to his he said sympathetically, 'It's a devil of a business just being tourists, isn't it?'

Fortunately he didn't seem to expect an answer. She stumbled once or twice on the long descent. Paul steadied her and teased her about taking more milk in her tea, and by the time they reached the bottom they'd laughed their way back into the easy friendliness that overcame any awkwardness between them.

It was late afternoon as they came out of the church. The sun was beginning to wane, but it was still warm as they walked down the steps between stretches of close-cropped grass to reach the bustle of Montmartre. 'Weary?' Paul asked, swinging her hand as though they were teenage sweetherts.

She felt like one as she replied, 'Nothing that putting my feet up for half an hour won't fix.'

'And I can depend on your being at the hotel at eight? Or do I have to arrive an hour earlier again?'

'I'll be there.'

Paul stopped swinging her hand and raised it to his lips to kiss. It was getting to be a habit, but one she was far from getting used to. Her heart constricted as emotion surged through her. She wanted to pull his hand to her lips to kiss. As she fought the impulse it came home to her how right he had been—it was the devil of a business just being tourists, and it was getting harder all the time.

Paul took her to a nightclub, as she'd suspected he might. She was wearing a red dress of fine jersey that wasn't quite right for the occasion, but she hadn't anything else remotely suitable except the dress she'd worn to the party. She yearned for silk or lace, but otherwise she knew she was looking her best.

Her black hair was parted in the middle and cascaded freely in a glossy sheen to below her shoulders. There was a glow about her that had nothing to do with make-up. It came from being with Paul. His eyes told her she was special, and that was enough.

They danced between courses and it was impossible to stay apart. Their bodies had a will of their own. They clung together like lovers' bodies, saying all the things Briony would have denied if Paul had forced her to put them into words. But Paul was being very careful not to force her into anything. Each time they returned to their table he kept the conversation to impersonal subjects, so that dancing together became dreamy interludes she could surrender to without worrying about the implications.

It wouldn't have worked with any other man, but Paul made it work, she wasn't sure how. In her more rational moments she realised she was being seduced at the same time as she was being treated like a valued friend. . .but she didn't have many rational moments.

When he took her back to the hotel he cupped her face in his hands and tilted her head up to his. 'Until tomorrow,' he murmured. 'It's going to seem a long time.'

Briony nodded. She'd drunk very little wine, but she felt intoxicated. She yearned to be in his arms and she stared at his lips, her lustrous eyes half closing in anticipation as she waited for him to kiss her. She sensed his yearning too, and it made the waiting all the sweeter.

Paul studied her for endless moments, then took his hands away and thrust them in his pockets. 'Sweet dreams,' he said, kissed her briefly on the forehead, and walked away.

Briony was bewildered. Her entire body was denied something it craved. She felt cheated, like a child robbed at the last moment of a promised treat, and the urge to burst into tears was almost over-whelming. It was almost as if Paul had dealt her a physical blow, and she could only stare at the glass doors swinging shut behind him.

There was nobody else in the foyer to read the disappointment on her face, but it wouldn't have made any difference if there had been. She was entirely defenceless as she watched Paul cross the pavement to the car. He paused, swung round and came swiftly back to her.

Briony began to breathe again, to live again, as the glass doors burst open and he swept her into his arms. He kissed her with a desperation that matched her own, their lips clinging and demanding more.

Finally he buried his face in her hair and said unsteadily, 'Heaven knows I've given it my best shot, but you and I can never be just tourists, my little love.'

Briony pressed her head into his shoulder, tears stinging her eyes. 'I know,' she breathed, 'but we've got to try. I have to be fair to Matthew. He's my fiancé. . .we shared our lives. . . I can't cheapen all that by jumping into bed with you when we've known each other such a little while.'

'Jumping into bed?' Paul repeated questioningly. 'Do you think that's all I'm interested in?'

Dear lord, how am I supposed to know? Briony wondered despairingly, Sheena's jibe about Paul only being interested in her because she was unavailable coming back to taunt her. Her instincts told her differently, and yet. . . She eased her head away from his shoulder and looked up at him appealingly.

She touched his face with loving fingers and closed her eyes as he caught and kissed them.

She said brokenly 'Paul, I feel as if I'm being pulled apart. I want to be with you, but I feel as though I still belong to Matthew. I need more time. . .to be absolutely certain. If you can't accept that, if you say you don't want to see me again, then I'll go anywhere with you—but I wouldn't be happy, I'd be guilty. You don't want that, do you?'

'You know I don't,' he said roughly, then frowned at her. 'Is this Matthew of yours one hell of a fellow, or are you the loyal type who goes down with the ship?'

'I'm a girl who's falling in love with you, and I'm frightened.'

His arms swept round her again and he hugged her to him. 'Don't be frightened, my darling, and don't worry. You can have whatever time we've got. I'll be so much of a tourist tomorrow I'll even bring my camera!'

Briony smiled mistily at him. 'That's funny, really. I never even thought to bring a camera. I wasn't thinking too straight when I packed.'

'You still aren't, but I love you anyway.' He kissed her on the forehead in the chaste way that had upset her a few minutes before, but this time she didn't mind. 'Sweet dreams,' he went on. 'I'm going now, or I won't be going at all.'

'Until tomorrow,' she said softly, and went upstairs in such a dream that it wasn't until she reached her room that she realised she'd forgotten the key. She had to go down again to get it, still very much in a dream. Paul had called her his little love and his darling, but now he'd actually said he loved her.

She yearned with every fibre of her being to believe him, and so she did. It didn't solve all her problems, but it helped her to shelve them for the next few days.

And the next few days were magical. Paul drove her out to the former royal palace at Versailles on Tuesday. As they crossed the cobbled square to enter the palace, the sun came out from behind the clouds and Paul posed her in front of a statue of Louis XIV on horseback and took a photograph. 'One for the family album,' he explained as they walked on.

Whose family? Briony wondered, believing he would think her a poor replacement for Sheena—if it came to that. She thrust the thought aside, as she was thrusting all disturbing thoughts aside, and gave herself over to the enjoyment of the day.

Hand in hand, they followed a guide around the vast palace, Briony awed by its opulence. When they came to the Galerie des Glaces, Paul smiled at her expression and said, 'I bet you've never seen anything quite as magnificent as this.'

She looked from the seventeen long windows to the seventeen corresponding mirrors and admitted, 'I don't think I have. It's not quite the same without a royal family, though, is it? I wouldn't mind applying to be queen!'

'Better learn to speak the language first,' Paul advised gravely.

Briony got the giggles and leaned her head against his shoulder as she struggled to get control of herself.

When she looked up at him, her face alight with laughter, the look in his eyes took her breath away. 'More petals unfurling,' he said softly. 'You're a different girl from the one I met on Sunday. You're getting more lovable all the time, and you were enchanting enough then.'

She was touched, but she didn't want to get serious. She and Paul were on pretty thin ice as it was and one wrong word could plunge them through. 'But not enchanting enough to be queen?' she answered lightly.

'Not of the French Republic. If you don't mind settling for plain Mrs you can always apply to me.'

Briony's heart missed a beat. She decided he must be teasing, and teased back, 'Do you always propose to all your women?'

'Only the pretty ones,' he answered promptly.

She laughed, glad they were back on their old easy footing, but the conversation remained at the back of her mind and came back to tease her in quiet moments. With Paul, though, she didn't have many of those. When they came out of the palace they wandered around the formal gardens and park for hours, happy in the sunshine and each other's company. She tried to think whether rain would have made any difference, but she couldn't concentrate. It just seemed so right that everything should be perfect for them.

'Hungry?' Paul asked at last.

'Is that your way of telling me you're starving?' When he laughed and nodded, she added, 'Good, because I am too.'

They drove out of Versailles, left the main road

and plunged into the countryside proper. 'Lovely!' Briony breathed. 'I always feel so at home in the country. Did I tell you that apart from my college years in Norwich and a few months in London, I've always been a proper rural hick?'

'You didn't use quite those words, but I got the message.'

'Here's another one for you,' she replied, looking at her watch. 'If we don't find a restaurant soon we'll be having afternoon tea, not lunch.'

'You're forgetting you're in France, and I know exactly where I'm heading. We'll be there in a couple of minutes.'

He stopped at a wayside *hostellerie* that didn't look much from the outside and Briony joked, 'I'd better warn you that if we're taking pot luck, I'm hungry enough to eat the pot.'

Paul grinned. 'You won't need to—the food's delicious. I've been here before.'

With Sheena? she wondered, and shrugged the thought away. She didn't want any spectres at the feast.

The restaurant-cum-bar was cosy and the hotelier made them welcome. For the first time Briony began to feel truly at home in France, and the strangeness of her and Paul being treated as a couple vanished as well. They'd known each other such a short space of time, and yet it was difficult to remember when she hadn't known him.

As they dined on mussels in parsley sauce, fillet steak with mushrooms, cheeses and fresh fruit, Briony was aware of a contentment she'd never experienced before. It felt so *right* being with Paul, and that in its own way was every bit as dangerous as the passion that could flare so quickly between them. She knew it, but she was helpless to do anything about it. She could only succumb to the enchantment of the moment, and try not to wonder whether a moment could stretch to a lifetime.

She was deeply, seriously in love—and she knew she couldn't play for time much longer.

After the meal Paul took her for a drive through the countryside. It was dark when they returned to her hotel and he asked, 'Can you be ready in an hour?'

'I can, but I couldn't possibly eat another heavy meal.'

'A light one, then, and lots of dancing.'

She nodded and raised her cheek for his kiss. It was impossible now to just walk away from him. Playing with fire, she was discovering, was making her dependent on its warmth, and it was a warmth that needed constant renewing.

They danced until two in the morning, and when they got back to her hotel the concierge wasn't in the television-room as usual. The top of his head was just visible above the high desk. 'He's asleep,' Paul whispered, and went behind the desk to get her key. 'Which one?'

'Thirty-two.'

He came back and gave it to her, his hand closing over hers as she took it. She looked up at him and then she was in his arms, their bodies moulding together as they did when they danced. It was hard, so very hard, to prise themselves apart. It was Paul who put her away from him finally. 'Until tomorrow at ten,' he said, in what was becoming a ritual.

Briony bit her lip, mutely appealing to be kissed.

'Don't do that,' he continued unsteadily. 'You should carry a warning—inflammable, store in a safe place!—and my arms are not a safe place.'

She reached up to him. Paul felt the coldness of the key against his cheek, the warmth of her hands and the swift fire of her lips against his. Then she broke from him and ran up the stairs.

He stared after her then began to follow. His hand was on the banister, his foot on the first stair, when he stopped. He stood there a long while, then turned abruptly and walked away.

# CHAPTER EIGHT

THEY were two days down and into the third. It seemed to Briony that wherever they went, a kind of feverishness went with them. They explored secret parts of Paris that never featured in the tourist guides, and still found time for the Louvre, the Catacombs, and everything else Paul thought she should see.

But no matter how much they packed into the precious hours together, Wednesday slipped into Thursday and Thursday raced into Friday. The more they tried to make time stand still, the faster it fled.

Late on Friday afternoon, Paul said, 'What time do you leave tomorrow?'

'Ten in the morning. And you?'

'I'm earlier. Seven.'

They were both silent. So few hours left, so much still unresolved between them. Paul had honoured his words and given her all the time available to make up her mind where her future lay, but time was running out. She had to make a decision—back into a known life with Matthew, or forward into the unknown with Paul.

He said, 'Our last night. I want you to myself. Will you come to the flat? I'll cook a meal.'

Briony didn't misunderstand. If she said 'yes' it would be to far more than a meal. So decision time

107

was here and now. Not later in her narrow bed as she tossed and turned and tried to sleep.

She tried to think of Matthew and the way they had once been, but she couldn't. Paul filled her eyes and her mind and her heart. There had never, she realised with new wisdom, been a decision to make. It had all been a question of how long she could delay making it.

And she could delay no longer.

'Briony?' Paul questioned softly.

With her whole future hanging on this moment it was a strange time for her shyness to reassert itself, but not for the life of her could she say 'yes'. Instead she asked, 'Can you cook?'

'Does it matter?'

She looked straight into his grey eyes and was lost. 'No,' she whispered. Then, as though to reassure herself, she said more positively, 'No.'

They were standing outside her hotel and home-bound commuters were pouring in and out of the nearby métro station. For all the notice Paul took of them they might have been alone. He kissed her softly on the lips, more as though he was claiming his own than demanding a commitment from her.

Briony melted, acknowledging his claim, only partly appreciating that he could be gentle with her because the commitment was already made.

'I'll call for you at seven,' he said, giving her another swift kiss, this time on the cheek, as they separated.

That was an hour earlier than ususal, but she understood. They simply hadn't any more hours to waste, and every second was wasted when they were apart.

He took her hand, kissed her palm and held on to her fingers until the last possible moment as she turned from him and went through the glass doors into the hotel foyer. This could only happen in Paris, she told herself, as she swivelled to wave to him, and then promptly knew that wasn't true.

Wherever or whenever she and Paul had met the outcome would have been the same. It was just that anywhere else in the world she might have fought a little harder.

Perhaps.

She booked a bath as she collected her key and went up to her room to inspect the few clothes she had hanging in her wardrobe. She wanted to wear something stunning, like Sheena's *couture* silk outfit on the night of the party, but there was nothing stunning there.

It would have to be the black dress again. She hadn't worn the barbaric earrings since the party, but she would wear them tonight. They were right for Paul's girl, and that made them appropriate. Tonight she would abandon Matthew. . .

Briony felt curiously detached as she bathed and dressed. Having made her decision, she felt absolved from it. What happened next was too inevitable to worry about. Excitement didn't begin to flicker beneath her surface calm until the hands of her watch approached seven o'clock.

Then her detachment crumbled. A glow rose to her cheeks and her limbs began to tremble. Getting married must be rather like this, she thought. But she wasn't getting married. The commitment, though, seemed the same.

Paul would come for her and she would go with him. She simply couldn't help herself. She didn't expect Matthew to understand, could scarcely understand herself. She just felt that what happened tonight was written long ago, perhaps at the dawn of time. She couldn't resist fate any longer.

Would anybody anywhere, she wondered, chalk up in her favour that she'd fought the inevitable for as long as she could? Did she even care? Her mind created a dynamic image of Paul. His grey eyes seemed to fill her soul and she knew that, no, she didn't care. Not tonight.

Not ever, she vowed, and shuddered almost in premonition. But there was a thrill in the shudder that the girl Paul had created couldn't resist. Matthew's girl would have been afraid—Paul's leapt to the challenge.

Briony stopped for a moment to study herself in the mirror. She'd used a soft charcoal shadow and liner to emphasise her eyes. The effect was sultry, mysterious. Her lipstick was pink, provocative. Matthew wouldn't recognise her, but Paul would. At last she was revealing the woman Paul had always suspected was there, the woman she was at last willing to become.

'Eat your heart out, Sheena,' she breathed, with new confidence. 'He's mine, and you'll never take him from me!'

It was on that high note that she went down the stairs to meet Paul. His gaze was swift, comprehensive. 'You look ravishing,' he said, unselfconsciously brushing his lips across hers under the interested eyes of the desk clerk.

Briony's stretched nerves tingled and dissolved into pleasure. Unthinkingly she dropped her key on the desk and succumbed to the strength of Paul's arm about her shoulders as he shepherded her out of the hotel.

'How's the cooking going?' she asked, feeling she had to say something as he settled her in the car.

'All bluff and short cuts, but don't worry, I won't let you starve.'

She laughed, and thought it strange that she could laugh, but Paul made everything so natural and easy for her. The thought came unbidden that perhaps he'd set the scene for seduction so many times that he was a past master of the art.

She brushed the thought aside as irrelevant. This was something she wanted. She simply couldn't believe she could crave a man who didn't love her. She wasn't that naïve or foolish.

'You've gone quiet,' Paul observed as he headed for the bridge over the Seine.

'I was just thinking that I've forgotten my indigestion tablets,' she replied, feeling frivolous and light-headed now that she'd finally managed to still all her nagging doubts.

She was rewarded by Paul's laughter, then they were parking on the quay outside the tall, gracious mansion. As he ushered her into the lift and took her up to the apartment she had a strange feeling of *déjà vu*, as though she'd always known she and Paul would be here again. Alone. Perhaps that was why she'd reacted so positively to Sheena, because she'd known she shouldn't be there. . .

The apartment was quiet, wrapping its gracious

atmosphere around them. She felt lulled, and yet self-conscious too. As Paul took her coat, she murmured, 'I can't smell cooking.'

'You will. I needed so much for you to come here that I wouldn't let myself believe you really would. I'm not normally superstitious, but I didn't dare anticipate too much. Can you understand that, or do you think I'm crazy?'

In her heightened awareness she understood only too well. She swayed towards him, her soft body reaching for the hardness of his. Demanding. . .

'Briony,' he breathed, his hands clasping her shoulders and running down the length of her supple spine to press her hips against his. 'My sweet Briony. . .'

She felt immediately that he was ready for her. She moved her hips against his in an instinctive, earthy response, never suspecting until this moment that she was capable of such abandon. Aeons of civilisation were peeling away from her, unleashing a wild primeval creature that took them both by surprise.

Paul gasped and unleashed his own passion. His mouth sought hers in a fever of desire. Her senses reeled as his long, sensuous kisses demanded her very soul and, unsated, sought for more.

Briony's back arched as he unzipped her dress and touched her bare flesh. The dress fell to the floor and he kicked it away. She unbuttoned his shirt and ran her hands over his matted chest, pressing her breasts into the dark hair in a frantic attempt to ease the ache in her hardened nipples.

It was her turn to gasp when he eased her away

and grasped her breasts, his strong fingers finding and holding her swollen nipples. He pinched and manipulated them until she felt dizzy with desire and began to bite him. They were swift, demanding nips, her teeth worrying his shoulders and chest as fire raged through her body. It was threatening to explode in her loins, but it was an explosion that wouldn't come, and she was punishing him for it.

Paul seized her up in his arms and carried her into the bedroom, laying her on a silk-covered bed and throwing himself down beside her. A new and delicious torture began as he sucked her breasts while he removed the last of their clothing. It was bare flesh against bare flesh now, and she explored and kneaded his body with feverish hands, transmitting urgency.

His lips moved over her, tantalising secret parts of her body until the fire that consumed her finally exploded. She cried out and he thrust into her, deeper and ever deeper, his power growing as hers ebbed.

When he climaxed she held him in his moment of triumph and cradled him against her as he collapsed. Neither of them spoke nor moved, their hearts still pounding, their minds and bodies united in an afterglow.

Briony's cheeks were wet with tears. She was in the grip of a new kind of ecstasy that came with complete fulfilment. She loved this man—heart, body and soul. The search that had begun with Matthew and moved on because of some deep inner dissatisfaction was over. She had found the man she'd been born for.

She made a small noise of protest when Paul finally eased himself away from her. She wanted them to stay like this forever. She wanted time to stand still. She wanted. . .oh, impossible things!

Paul looked down at her with a tenderness that made their separation bearable. He kissed her wet cheeks, brushed the tumbled hair away from her face and murmured, 'I think I've been raped.'

A tender smile touched her own lips. All restraint and shyness was gone now. She could be herself now, the Briony Spenser he'd revealed rather than created. 'Was it so terrible?' she asked mischievously.

'It was——' he paused, seeking the right words '—out of this world. I think we touched the stars.'

'You might have done. I went way past them.'

Paul laughed and traced her lips with gentle fingers, the fire gone from them now, but she didn't need fire any more. 'Have I shown you how much I love you?' he asked. 'Do you understand now why I couldn't let you go when we first met? One look and I wanted you more than I've ever wanted any other woman. As I always will.'

It had all happened so fast Briony didn't know if she could believe in perfect happiness. She was seized with doubt and replied anxiously, 'Even though there are no petals left to unfurl?'

'There'll always be new petals with you, my little love. You never cease to surprise and delight me.'

Her anxiety faded away. 'I love you so very much,' she whispered.

He kissed her. 'The time and effort it's taken to drag that out of you!'

'Less than a week,' she protested, 'and I did have other things on my mind.'

Paul silenced her with another kiss, then he stood up and gathered her into his arms, 'We're not going to talk about those "other things" just now.'

'Oh? What are we going to do?'

'Shower, cook, eat. . .'

Briony wound her arms around his neck, totally unashamed of her nakedness. 'We've done everything the wrong way round, haven't we?'

'No,' he replied, carrying her into the bathroom. 'This way we can make love all over again.'

'But that wasn't the way you planned, was it?'

'No,' he repeated. 'As I've just said, you constantly surprise and delight me.'

'I was afraid you might get bored with me. I'm nothing very special.'

Paul looked down at her in amazement. 'Believe me, Briony, you are very, very special. I thought I knew it all, but you've proved me wrong. I shall expect to be raped at least once a day for the rest of my life.'

She discovered she wasn't so very different, after all, because she blushed and tried to hide her head in his shoulder.

Paul laughed, dumped her in the shower and stepped in with her. He switched on the taps, and as the water gushed over them he said, 'It's too late for modesty now. I know what sort of a beast lurks behind those blushes.'

Briony growled at him. It was the wrong, or the right, thing to do, because they made love again much sooner than they intended.

When they were wrapped in towelling robes and Briony had borrowed Chantal's drier for her hair, they eventually wandered hand in hand into the kitchen. 'I hope it's something simple,' she said. 'I'm hungry, but I don't feel like making much effort.'

'It's dead simple. Prawn cocktails already in the fridge. Kebabs already marinading. Salad already prepared. Wine already cooling. Table already set.'

'That's a lot of "alreadys". You have been busy,' she commented.

'I didn't want to waste any time better used in seducing you, but you made that unnecessary.'

'I'm never going to live that down, am I?' But Briony's smile faded a little as she added, 'Was it so important—seduction, I mean? Wouldn't it have been enough if we'd just told each other of our love?'

Paul shook his head, his own face serious. 'I needed to make you mine. For one thing, I couldn't bear you belonging to another man. For another, I couldn't be sure you'd let him go unless you committed yourself to me. You're a very loyal creature and I won't be easy until I'm certain all your loyalty is mine. I need *everything* about you to be mine.'

She placed her fingers across his lips in a pacifying gesture, touched that he could sound so fierce and be so unsure after what had happened between them. 'I'm all yours,' she insisted. 'Heart, mind, body and soul.'

'That will do for starters,' he said, and caught her once more into his arms.

They were slow to get the kebabs under the grill, unable to let each other go for more than a minute at a time, but eventually they dined by candlelight, their fingers touching constantly across the table.

It all seemed like a dream to Briony. Then she remembered Paul saying way back at the beginning, 'I deal in hard facts. The dreams I leave to others.' She felt a little chill, an icy finger of doubt touching her spine, and remembered other things. Herself knowing instinctively that he was a man who always got what he wanted. . .a taxi in the rain. . .a girl in his bed.

'Paul. . .'

'Yes, darling?'

'That first lunch we had together. You proposed a toast to my wedding. How could you do that if you didn't want me to marry Matthew?' she asked.

'The toast was to your wedding. I didn't say who to.'

'Oh.' She hadn't thought of that, but she couldn't be easy. 'You said you'd tell me why I shouldn't marry Matthew. . .when I was ready. I'm as ready now as I'm ever going to be.'

Once more his hand came across the table, not to touch her fingers this time but to clasp them firmly. 'He came into your life at a time when you needed somebody to love, and somebody to love you. I don't doubt the love seemed real enough for a little while, but it was based on insecurity and dependency. It was a girl's love, and you've outgrown it. You're a woman now, capable of love on an equal footing, and so much of you was still unfulfilled. You didn't know what was missing, but that's why you ran away—to look for it.'

'And I said I didn't come to Paris for a tatty adventure,' she breathed.

'If you call this a tatty adventure——' Paul's grip on her fingers became cruel as his temper flared. Briony winced and immediately the pressure eased. He was still angry, though, as he continued, 'Don't tell me you're still having doubts!'

'No,' she said hastily, 'but if we love each other surely we can talk about these things rationally?'

'We can try, if you allow for my jealous nature.' He was kissing her mangled fingers. 'I'm sorry if I hurt you, but I can't bear to share even your thoughts with somebody else.'

Briony was thrilled he cared so much for her and her doubts disappeared. She pulled his hand towards her lips and kissed his fingers. 'You've told me more than once to trust you. Well, you have to trust me too.'

Paul smiled and replied ruefully, 'You have the most devastating habit of throwing my own words back in my face.'

'But you trust me?' she insisted.

'Implicitly. After all, I have your promise that you'll never marry for anything but love.'

'That was more than a promise,' she replied, recalling it. 'It was a vow.'

'Then we don't have any problems, do we?'

Briony shook her head, although she still had several. But she would cope with them. Paul's love would make her strong, help her find the right words to make Matthew understand. She would tell him straight out because the quicker it was done the better. There was no way she could make Matthew happy now and, once he realised that, he would let her go. He was too nice to do otherwise.

Oh, hell, she wished Matthew weren't so nice!

When she went to bed with Paul again they lay in each other's arms a long while, luxuriating in a feeling of unity that had nothing to do with passion. They both knew that would come later, and in the meantime this euphoria had its own kind of bliss.

'When will I see you again?' Briony asked, running a hand across his shoulder and down the length of his arm, fascinated by the strength and maleness of his body.

'I'll be in London the second week in June. I'll pick you up and we'll go to New York together. We'll sort out the details later.'

'Three months!' she sighed. 'But we'll write?'

'I'll phone you first, to let you know where I am and when I actually get to Hong Kong.'

Briony raised herself on her elbow to look down at him. How handsome he was, this man she'd met by such a crazy chance. And he was hers, all hers. It was still so hard for her to believe. Perhaps that was why she was never quite free of doubts. 'Don't you know?' she asked incredulously.

'It's not a straight flight. I'm stopping off at our various agencies on the way to do a bit of checking— managerial work.'

'I hate to think of you out of touch.'

'I'll phone you as soon as I can.' He smiled at her anxious face above him, pulled her head down and breathed against her lips, 'Probably tomorrow night.'

She was reassured, but said, 'I might not be at the

hotel. I have to sort things out with Matthew. I'm not on duty Sunday and personal calls are frowned on. Make it Monday—I'm due on day shift.'

'Monday it is, then, so long as you promise not to stop thinking of me between now and then.'

She promised, and he heaved himself up, rolling her on her back, his loving kisses becoming more urgent as passion awoke once more between them. Already there was a familiarity between them, a knowledge that was infinitely more precious than the novelty with which they'd first made love. It just grew and grew, this love she had for Paul, and so did the passion and the fulfilment.

They slept in each other's arms, something Briony had never found comfortable before, but even in their sleep their bodies seemed to gravitate towards each other. Briony awoke first. The bedside lamp was still on and carefully she reached to switch it off.

She was left in the dark world of pre-dawn, but in their absorption in each other they'd forgotten to close the curtains and a certain amount of dying moonlight allowed her to see Paul's tousled head on the pillow beside her. How deeply he slept, and how strong he looked, even in his sleep. Briony felt a great surge of love for him and she bent gently to kiss his hair.

Then she lay back on her own pillow, her eyes turning involuntarily towards the windows. Only the frilled net curtains shrouded their privacy, enclosing them in a temporary paradise. She moved restlessly, she wasn't sure why—unless it was because the white net seemed such a fragile barrier against the outside world.

The moonlight could intrude. . .and so did her thoughts. Poor Matthew, he didn't deserve what she was going to do to him. Had already done. She looked at Paul and her anxiety abated. She couldn't be held responsible for something that was inevitable, irresistible.

Could she?

She shifted restlessly again, her eyes roving around the room. It was one of those deceptively uncluttered rooms where each item cost a fortune and lasted forever. Understated luxury, a new world Paul had swept her into, and to which she hadn't properly adjusted yet.

His suitcases were already packed and by the door. Very expensive leather. He would probably use them all his life, while her holdall was already falling apart after two years. Briony gave her head a little shake. Her mind was wandering, anywhere and everywhere rather than face up to the fact that in a very short while she and Paul would be parting.

She knew he'd set the alarm, but it was on his side of the bed and she couldn't see it. Did they have an hour, two hours? She didn't know. It might only be minutes. Out of nowhere, Chantal's voice came back to her: 'Don't waste those days; you might never have any as precious again.'

Superstitiously afraid, Briony snuggled down and pressed her body as close to Paul's as she could. He murmured in his sleep and his arm moved from her hips to her waist and tightened. She nuzzled her cheek against his, reassured. They might have to part, but nothing would really separate them. They loved each other. . .

Her eyes closed and she slept again. Neither of them stirred until the alarm shrilled them into wakefulness. Paul had set it to the last moment so they could have as long as possible together, and now they were both galvanised into a frantic rush.

They showered together, dressed, grabbed coffee, and then a bell pierced their private little world. 'The taxi,' Paul said, and opened his arms. Briony walked into them and clung, feeling his mouth on her hair, her forehead, her cheeks, searching for her lips.

She raised them, her eyes closing, knowing there was not enough time. . .that there would never be enough time for her and Paul. Then they were in the quaint old lift and the modern taxi, the intrigued driver watching them most of the time in his rear mirror.

But this was Paris where love was understood, and Briony didn't feel the least embarrassed as she clung to Paul on the brief journey to her hotel, her head on his shoulder, his arm around her. When they arrived he said, 'When you see Matthew again, you won't. . .?'

She silenced him with her lips. 'You don't have to worry—I'll tell him right away.'

He looked deep into her eyes and what he saw there seemed to satisfy him. 'I'll phone you at the hotel on Monday. Be there.'

'I will,' she promised. She knew there was barely time for him to get to the airport to catch his flight, so she wrenched herself away from him. It was the hardest thing she'd ever done in her life. She jumped out of the taxi, slammed the door behind her and stood waving until it was lost from her view.

She went into the hotel and took her key from the concierge, impervious to his knowing smile. Everything paled into insignificance compared to Paul speeding away from her. Three whole months. However would she get through them?

In her room she packed, checked that her passport and tickets were in her handbag, then sat by the window. Eventually she heard people going down to breakfast. She didn't join them. She sat on, watching the stray cats roaming around the car park waiting for the first car to arrive.

Around nine o'clock, one did. Briony watched the cats jump up on the bonnet, manoeuvre for position, then snuggle down. She stood up, slung her handbag over her shoulder and grasped the handles of her holdall. She had a very unpleasant task facing her, but her love for Paul strengthened her and she felt equal to it.

She checked out of the hotel and walked purposefully towards the métro. Her Paris adventure was over. The rest of her life would begin when Paul came to London to claim her.

# CHAPTER NINE

THERE was a 'Do Not Disturb' notice hanging from the door-handle when Briony reached her room at the back of Dabell's Hotel. She crept in, closed the door silently and trod softly across the flat blue carpet to put her holdall down on the bed.

Wearily she sat down next to it. The journey home hadn't gone with the clockwork efficiency of the journey out. For some reason she'd never discovered, the train had been diverted from Boulogne to Calais. She'd become impatient of its meanderings, and when she'd finally boarded the hovercraft the journey had been bumpy.

To crown it all, she'd been picked out at Customs and had her bag searched, and all the time she'd known that every mile she gained was taking her further and further away from Paul.

But her weariness was all mental and physical. Emotionally she was still safely wrapped in the cosy cocoon of her and Paul's love. She sighed and her eyes travelled to the fair hair just visible above the huddle of blankets on the opposite bed. Donna Thompson, her friend and fellow receptionist, was well tucked down. Poor darling, she must have been on night duty.

Weary as she was, Briony didn't feel like sleeping herself. She had one last hurdle to leap between herself and happiness before she could let her head hit the pillow. Matthew had to be told, made to understand.

Involuntarily she looked at the framed photograph on her bedside table. Matthew, snapped just before he'd gone to the States. His was a pleasant, trustworthy face—honest blue eyes, sensitive mouth, fair hair neatly brushed back from his forehead.

As different from Paul as it was possible to be. . .

Briony felt a momentary qualm, but the sheer power of her love for Paul overcame it. Matthew was flying in this evening, and it was this evening she would tell him. She wouldn't—couldn't!—delay, not for all their sakes.

She stood up and began to unpack. It was best to keep busy, not to think—just to act—and her first act was to prop in front of Matthew's photograph the snap of herself and Paul.

She studied it, remembering that blissful day on the Seine, the laughter, the feel of Paul's arm around her shoulders. One memory led to another and she sat down again, lost in a different world. All due to Paul, of course. He'd turned fact into fantasy, and fantasy into fact. And, dear heaven, how she loved him. . .

It was at that moment she saw the note on her pillow. Smiling, she reached for it, not doubting that this was Donna's way of welcoming her home. She was full of nice impulses like that.

Impulses, Briony thought, and smiled again.

Her smile faded as she read the note. Her fingers stiffened on the flimsy paper as a deepening chill turned her to ice. One part of her brain recalled the premonitions she'd had in Paris, the subconscious feeling that for her and Paul time had always been running out.

The other part of her brain clung to hope, needing to believe she was panicking over nothing. When she got to the end of the note, she read it again.

'Sorry to let you know this way,' Donna had written, 'but Matthew is seriously ill in hospital. Apparently he managed to get an earlier flight and collapsed as he arrived yesterday evening. The ward sister phoned and said please would you get in touch urgently.'

Carefully printed below was the name of the hospital, the ward and the phone number.

Briony reached for her handbag and the photograph. Carefully she tucked it back inside like a talisman, proof of how happy she and Paul had been. Then she went out and hailed a taxi. She felt quite numb. The feeling of disbelief still clung to her as the ward sister led her into a side room and asked her to wait while she called Matthew's doctor.

Eventually he arrived, a calm-looking man in his late thirties. He took one look at her rigid face and asked an orderly to bring in tea. He chatted quietly while they were waiting for it. Briony was incapable of bringing him to the point. She still couldn't believe—didn't want to believe!—that any of this was happening.

It was only after he'd insisted she drink the tea that he began to tell her. Briony listened, not really taking it in, until he said, 'We're operating tomorrow.'

'On a Sunday?' It was a silly thing to say, but she couldn't think of anything else.

'The tumour is growing so rapidly we'd have operated today if he'd let us, but he wanted to see you first. That's why he refused an operation in the States when it was first diagnosed.'

'Dear lord!' Briony whispered. 'I would have flown out to him if I'd known.' But she hadn't known, and so she'd gone to Paris and fallen in love with Paul. She remembered the passion of last night, but it was with a poignancy that seared her to the bone. She sensed that Paul was slipping away from her and frantically she tried to hang on to him.

'He wanted to come home,' the doctor said gently. 'People do, you know, if they think they're dying.'

Dying. . .dear, gentle Matthew. It was so cruel, so unfair. 'But he's not, is he? I mean, there's a chance. . .' Her voice trailed away. She still couldn't come to terms with the fact that Matthew—brilliant Matthew!—had a tumour on the brain.

'There would have been a good chance if he'd sought help when he first realised something was wrong, but Matthew is a very single-minded young man. He was determined to complete his studies and then come home and marry you. He was sure there'd be time, you see.'

'And now?' Briony breathed.

'I won't lie to you. His general medical history isn't good. I assume you know about that?'

'I know he had a kidney disease when he was a child, but I thought he was over that,' she faltered.

'It left him with one useless kidney and the other damaged. We wouldn't operate if we could possibly avoid it, but if we don't he'll die anyway,' the doctor told her.

Briony's mind reeled. 'Why didn't he tell me. . .?'

'Young men have their pride. They like to seem as macho as the next man.'

'But we were so close!' It was almost an accusation, and blindly she looked at the doctor. From somewhere within her a different kind of compassion stirred. This couldn't be easy for him either. 'I'm sorry,' she added. 'I was in such a state when the sister brought you in I didn't catch your name.'

'That's all right. It's Preston.'

'You're his surgeon?' When he nodded, she went on, 'You'll be Mr, then, not Dr Preston. What can I do to help?'

He gave her an assessing look, made up his mind, and replied, 'I'll be frank. The only thing Matthew's got going for him is his will to live, and you're a part of it. He wants to marry you immediately. We've got a special licence and the padre is on standby. I know it won't be the wedding you've envisaged, with all the frills and flowers, but. . .'

His voice trailed off and hung in the air between them. 'Of course,' she heard herself say.

Mr Preston touched her arm, but the warmth of human contact was something she couldn't react to. It didn't pierce the ice that was encasing her, the despair. By marrying Matthew she would be renouncing Paul, and she couldn't do that. Later, when Matthew was strong again, she would explain why she could never truly be his wife. She would explain to Paul too.

They'd both understand, wouldn't they? She had to believe they would. It was wrong to say there was always a choice. This time there wasn't, not for her.

'Sister will take you through to Matthew,' Mr Preston said, standing up.

The interview that had shattered her life was over. Briony stood up as well, like an automaton. If only she could phone Paul now, let him know what was happening, but he was out of reach. She hadn't even the vaguest clue where he was. He would have to trust her, just as she'd had to trust him.

Mr Preston was still studying her carefully. He said, 'You'll have to be brave, Briony, keep your fears to yourself. Matthew needs to see you bright and smiling and confident. He needs to know all the time that he has every reason to live. I know how you must be feeling, but you must suppress all that and concentrate on him.'

She nodded, although Mr Preston actually had no idea how she was feeling. Nobody could. Except, perhaps, Paul.

Oh, Paul, her heart cried, where are you?

But when she walked into the ward and looked down at Matthew, her lips were smiling. He didn't seem so very different. A little thinner, perhaps, but then he'd always been thin.

In those seconds it all rushed over her how much she owed to him—the way he'd cared for her when there'd been nobody else. . .built up her confidence with his love. . .made her a whole person.

'Hello, you shirker,' she said cheerfully. 'If this is all a confidence trick to get out of marrying me, you've wasted your time.'

Matthew's dear face lit up. He opened his arms and Briony bent into them. She could feel tears stinging her eyes. Tears for Matthew and, because she wasn't as noble as she would like to be, tears for herself. She didn't need to cry for Paul, she persuaded herself. A vision of his strong face swam before her eyes and nothing would wash it away.

Like their love, she thought. And believed it.

An hour later, she and Matthew were married. The nurses and doctors were marvellous, turning the brief ceremony into a festive occasion. They didn't know Briony was looking at the simple gold band encircling her finger as though it were somebody else's ring. Even somebody else's finger. Reality had trapped her again, truly trapped her.

Somewhere out there the world was spinning uncaringly on its eternal journey around the sun. Somewhere out there was Paul, and he still didn't know she was somebody else's wife.

The hotel did. She'd phoned and explained. She'd asked for leave, then for a careful record of any messages that came in for her. It was very awkward. She was Mrs Matthew Hammond now, and she couldn't very well explain her dependency on a call from Mr Paul Deverill.

She spent the night by Matthew's bedside. She held his hand and listened to his plans for their future. He was so certain there was going to be a future, and she had to be certain as well. It was more than her duty, it was her wish. She desperately wanted Matthew to live. She had a kind of love for him and she always would.

Paul would have to understand about that too. Perhaps he already did—and called it loyalty. Perhaps he was right. Briony was too shattered to work it out properly. She could only sit there holding Matthew's hand, giving him all the affection she could and making it seem like the love he deserved.

But she felt such a traitor—to Matthew, Paul and herself.

She was offered a bed for the night, but she refused, wanting to stay with Matthew, wanting even more to make up for all the things she could never make come out right. Matthew needed her and she needed Paul. Life played such cruel tricks.

In the morning there was such little time for all the last-minute things she wanted to say to Matthew to make him fight for life, and it was so hopeless anyway when she had to appear cheerful and confident. Strangely, it was Matthew who was strong and cheerful and confident.

'Well done!' the sister whispered to her as Matthew was wheeled away. 'You've given him every reason to live, and that's what is so important.'

Briony only nodded. She felt drained and sat down again for the long wait. She took out the photograph of herself and Paul, lovingly touched his smiling face and then put it away again. She was Mrs Matthew Hammond, and that was her husband fighting for his life in the operating theatre.

It didn't seem real. When it became real, she didn't know whether she'd be able to cope.

Matthew survived the operation. Briony was allowed to sit beside him in Intensive Care. She was beginning to hope, daring to see the light at the end of the tunnel. It would be several weeks, but eventually he would be strong again—strong enough for her to explain why she'd married him but could never be his wife.

He would release her and Paul would wait. Her heart constricted a little in panic, because Paul wasn't a patient man. Then her breathing eased. Paul was different now. He was a man in love, and love could be very patient when it had to be.

Sunday night passed, and on Monday, during those times when Matthew was conscious, she talked to him of all the things he wanted to hear. She concentrated totally on him, shutting out from her mind that today Paul would be phoning her at the hotel, holding Matthew's hand and willing all her life-force into his.

She knew with every hour that passed his chances of survival were growing stronger. It was—it had to be—enough.

Just before dawn on Tuesday morning Matthew died. His collapse was sudden and caught Briony totally unprepared. She'd been prepared on Sunday. . .on Monday. . .but not now, when she'd convinced herself the worst was over.

She went into shock and knew little about being led away, sedated and put to bed. It wasn't until Wednesday that she could think and feel and act again. Instinctively she went back to the hotel. It was the only home she knew, and Paul's message would be waiting. Dear lord, how much she needed his strength now!

Dabell's was a large, gracious hotel and she was only a small cog in it, but the manager was sympathetic and offered her extended leave. Briony refused.

Work was the best therapy—she had Paul and Chantal's word for that. She asked if she could begin immediately and just have Monday off for the funeral.

She could see old Mr Mathers, who'd been the manager for the past thirty years, looking at her strangley. 'You know best, Mrs Hammond,' he said at last with his quaint old-world formality. 'I can't deny we're short-staffed, but if you find it's all too much just let me know. We'll carry on managing somehow.'

She thanked him and hurried to her room. Donna was sleeping, so her night tour couldn't be over. Briony went straight to her pillow for the message she knew must be there. It wasn't, and even a search under her pillow failed to find it. She was disappointed, but she wasn't worried. Paul's message must still be in Reception.

She changed hurriedly into the cream blouse and brown skirt that was her uniform and swiftly tamed her hair into a neat French pleat. Her fingers trembled slightly as she remembered Paul liked it to fall loosely past her shoulders. Paul, she thought, and found new strength. Their love was the one rock left in her life she could lean on, the rock that was keeping her going.

Her holdall had vanished from the bed to a shelf in her wardrobe. Donna had unpacked for her, even laundered her clothes and put them away. Everybody was being so kind, and tears stung her eyes.

She blinked them away, conscious all the time of Matthew's photograph still on her bedside table. At last she picked it up and studied his dear face, almost overcome. Then, with a resolution her love for Paul gave her, she put it away in a drawer. Nobody would understand why, not even Donna who was her closest friend.

But Donna hadn't heard the last words Matthew had said to her before he'd been sedated for the operation: 'Whatever happens, Briony, be happy. Promise me. I can bear anything except your being sad.'

She'd promised, awed by the depth of his love for her, and feeling even more unworthy. A kind of calm had come to her later, though, during her long vigil at his bedside. She'd realised love was a force outside human control, and neither she nor Paul nor Matthew could be held responsible for who or how they loved. It just happened. Once she'd accepted that the guilt had lifted. It was almost as if she'd been given an absolution.

With a mammoth effort Briony tried to brush the past aside. She had to think of the future, and Paul was her future.

Impelled by a need for even the slightest contact with him, she hurried to Reception to find his message. She was greeted with sympathy that only thinly overlaid the relief of the under-manager, Bryan Stockton, who was one of the people who'd been covering for her.

As soon as she could, she asked, 'Are there any messages for me?'

Bryan was already lifting the flap to leave the long reception desk, but he looked back and replied, 'No. Should there be?'

She nearly screamed at him, 'Yes, there should!'

but she managed to clench her hands and control herself. After a moment she said, 'I thought there might have been a phone call.'

'No, nothing.' Bryan frowned, showing real concern. 'Should there have been?'

'No—no. . .' she denied. 'I just wondered.'

'Oh, well—look, Briony, if you can't cope——'

'I'll be fine,' she cut in. 'Thanks, Bryan, but I need to work.'

He hesitated a moment longer, then nodded. 'Just call me if you need me,' he said, and left her to her thoughts.

They were frantic, but with a very positive effort she managed to calm them down. Paul couldn't have left a message because he intended to call again. Any moment the phone would ring, she'd hear his beloved voice and her reeling world would straighten.

The phone never stopped ringing, but it was never Paul. Briony told herself it was because he was somewhere completely out of touch, that he *couldn't* phone, or the lines were down or. . . She made up a million different excuses for him, believing every one because she couldn't bear *not* to believe them.

It was too early in the year for spring visitors to fill the hotel, but fortunately there was a lavish exhibition on in London that kept the hotel almost fully booked. Briony was kept very busy. She worked efficiently, an automaton again, neither her face nor her voice revealing her inner turmoil.

She almost lost her grip on herself when Donna came on duty and exclaimed, 'Briony, are you crazy? What are you doing working? You must be——'

'Don't!' Briony broke in. 'Please don't say a word about Matthew. I just couldn't take it.'

'Of course not, you poor darling,' Donna replied instantly, 'but I feel so helpless. Isn't there anything I can do? Anything any of us can do?'

Briony shook her head. 'You don't understand, nobody does, but I can't talk about it now. Later. . .'

These cryptic utterances seemed to make more sense to her friend than they did to herself, because Donna said swiftly, 'Whenever you're ready, I'll be there.'

'Thank you.' Briony felt dazed again, trying to recall how many times she'd said those two words over the past few days. When people were kind it was polite to say 'thank you', even when nothing they did or said could even begin to help.

Yet again she pulled herself together and said, 'There's just one thing, Donna. Has anybody phoned me over the past few days?'

'Not while I've been on duty, and there hasn't been anything for you on the message pad. I've kept a careful check.'

Briony felt her heart grow cold, a new kind of coldness, as for the first time she allowed the possibility that Paul wasn't going to contact her seep through the pathetic barrier she had built around herself. She swallowed and tried to smile as she said, 'If anybody does, you'll buzz through for me, won't you? Whatever time of the night?'

Donna looked concerned. 'For heaven's sake, you need whatever sleep you can get, you poor thing.'

'Just do it!' Briony exclaimed, her voice almost rising out of control. Then she walked away.

She was shaking when she reached her room. There was a wickerwork armchair in one corner which she and Donna laughingly fought over on those rare occasions when they were off duty together. Briony sat in it, hugging herself to stop her violent trembling and contain her rising fears.

She'd been through so much, she really couldn't take any more. Paul had promised—*promised!*—to phone her on Monday, and it was Wednesday evening. All those excuses she'd dreamed up earlier were wearing thin from revolving endlessly around her brain. All she could think of now was how positive he was about everything. He was a man who made things happen. He'd have found a way to get in touch if he'd really wanted to—if not on Monday, then certainly by now.

She hugged and rocked herself, then slowly her alarm subsided and her shivering ceased. She was remembering how she and Paul had been together. All that love, ever-growing waves of it, sweeping them off their feet into a personal paradise. She was safe in such a love. She'd known it then and, as she was thinking rationally again, she knew it now.

Paul would phone tonight. He would be driven, just as she was being driven, by an aching need to speak to each other again. He wouldn't delay a moment longer then necessary.

Feeling so much calmer, Briony changed from her uniform into casual clothes so that she could dash through to Reception when Donna buzzed through on the staff intercom for her. She sat down in the armchair to wait. As she relaxed, the trauma and weariness of the past days crept over her. Her eyes were closing of their own volition and nothing she could do would keep them open.

She lay down fully clothed on her bed, the photograph of herself and Paul in her hand. It was all she had of him and she couldn't let it go. She pulled the quilt up to her hips and snuggled her head into the pillow. She would just rest for a little while until Paul phoned. . .

That was how Donna found her when she came off duty early the next morning. She stood looking down at Briony and reached gently to pull the quilt up to her shoulders. She paused as she saw the photograph that had slipped from Briony's fingers. It was a little crumpled, and she smoothed it out before she studied it.

She didn't know the man, but he had his arm around Briony's shoulders and Briony looked so happy. Radiant. Puzzled, Donna put the photograph on the bedside table and noticed that the framed portrait of Matthew had gone.

It was then that Briony stirred. She looked up blankly at Donna for a few seconds. She was fighting her way back to full consciousness through cloying layers of sleep, but she still had the same thought on her mind she'd fallen asleep with. She grasped Donna's hand and said, 'Has he phoned?'

'Oh, you poor darling, you've been dreaming,' Donna replied, her voice brimming with compassion. 'Matthew can't phone. He's—he's——'

'Not Matthew—Paul! He must have phoned. Why didn't you call me? I told you to, you know I did.'

'Paul?' Donna echoed, baffled. 'Who's he? Don't

upset yourself, you haven't missed anything.
Nobody phoned for you.'

Briony's lips trembled, her eyes filled with tears
and she began to hunt around the bed. Donna stared
at her in alarm, sat down on the bed and began to
smooth Briony's tangled hair back from her forehead. 'You just lie there like a good little lamb and
I'll call a doctor,' she soothed. 'It's all been too
much for you, and who can wonder?'

'I don't want a doctor! I want my photograph!'

She sounded on the edge of hysteria, and Donna
hurriedly gave her the snap she'd retrieved from the
bed. 'Do you mean this one?'

Briony grabbed it and sat up. She stared at it as
though it were her whole world, then raised
anguished eyes to her friend. 'It's all crumpled up.'
Her voice wobbled as she went on, 'It's spoilt! Oh,
Donna, it's all spoilt—everything!'

She burst into tears. Donna hugged and soothed
her and, when the first wild storm had passed, drew
the whole story out of her with gentle questioning.
'Well, I always did say you tied yourself to one man
too soon,' she said at last. 'You mustn't blame
yourself for what happened. It was inevitable.'

'That's what I told myself.' Briony had stopped
sobbing and achieved a degree of calm, but her
anguish remained with her. 'I kidded myself it was
all right because Paul and I loved each other. But he
hasn't phoned, and he promised he would. He
*promised*!'

Sheena warned me, she thought. She'd spelled it
out loud and clear: 'He tramples all over little girls
who fall at his feet. . .' Briony closed her eyes as a

fresh wave of anguish swept over her. She felt as though the whole world had trampled over her in the past few days. It was Paul who mattered, though. Only Paul. . .

'I was nothing but a challenge to him,' she whispered. 'I was engaged to somebody else and tried to brush him off. That's what made me irresistible.'

'You don't know that. You're only guessing. Trust what you felt at the time—and you felt that he loved you, didn't you?'

'Oh, yes!' Briony fumbled for the box of tissues on the bedside table and blew her nose. Donna's calm good sense was beginning to get through to her. She'd needed so much to cry the trauma of the past few days out of her, and she was starting to feel better. Just a bit.

'You could very well have been right when you thought Paul was stranded somewhere out of touch,' Donna went on, relieved to see Briony was losing her ghastly pallor. 'The agency's bound to know where his next point of contact is. Why don't you phone them to find out?'

'No.' Briony's confidence in Paul's love for her was coming back, and with it came rational thinking. 'Paul told me more than once that I must trust him. With the kind of life he leads the last thing he needs is a hysterical female on the phone every five minutes.'

Sheena, she was thinking, would never be hysterical.

'It's been rather longer than five minutes,' Donna said drily, 'and in this particular instance you do have a right to be hysterical.'

'No, I don't,' Briony replied sadly. 'I knew exactly what I was doing when I betrayed Matthew. If he'd recovered I would still have shattered him. That's something I have to live with, not Paul. It was a personal decision. I wasn't over-persuaded.' She flung the quilt back and swung her legs out of bed. 'And I'm going to start living with it now. I love Paul and he loves me. He'll get in touch—I know it! Meanwhile, I need a shower. I'm on duty in an hour.'

'Briony, you're not thinking of working today!'

'What's the alternative? To sit around here moping? No, thanks!'

So Briony went back on duty, buoyed up by the belief that any moment Paul would surface and get in touch. She went through Thursday and Friday like that, then staggered through the weekend. Day by day, hour by hour, her confidence was whittled away. Monday was Matthew's funeral. Donna went with her. It was harrowing, and yet strangely unreal. Briony felt as though she were burying a very dear friend, not a husband. The gold ring on her finger had no relevance.

In spirit and in body she was Paul's wife. Paul. . .who still hadn't backed up his claim on her.

When they got back to their room, Donna said, 'For heaven's sake phone the agency, find out where he is and why he hasn't called. You can't go on like this. You're wasting away.'

'With Matthew just buried? It doesn't seem right.'

'You did your best for Matthew while he was alive. Now he's gone. You're still here, and so is Paul—somewhere. Find him and start living again.'

Briony turned a piteous face to her. 'But he told me to trust him!'

'And do you—still?'

Briony looked down at her hands twisting nervously in her lap. Then she picked up her handbag and went to the pay phone along the passage. She looked the agency's number up in the book and dialled.

Mr Paul Deverill, she learned, had been at the Hong Kong office since Saturday and no, there was nothing wrong with communications. He was in regular touch with the head office. Briony felt as though she were standing back watching herself as she asked for the number of the Hong Kong office and wrote it down.

When she replaced the receiver she stood looking at the number for a long while. She didn't want to call it. She was too afraid of confirming what, deep down, she already knew.

# CHAPTER TEN

DONNA came looking for Briony, worry lines creasing her youthful face. 'Briony, you've been an age! What on earth are you doing just standing here? Couldn't you get through to the agency?'

'Yes, I got through. Paul's in Hong Kong, and has been since Saturday.'

Their eyes met. They were both thinking the same thing. Two whole days to make contact from Hong Kong and he hadn't bothered. 'It doesn't look too good, does it?' Briony said at last, trying to smile and failing abysmally. 'I've got his Hong Kong number, but I'm not going to phone it. It's—it's over, and I'm going to accept that.'

'Well, I'm not. You have to know for certain, one way or the other. The bastard owes you that much, at least.' Donna took the slip of paper with Paul's number on, fed coins into the box, punched out the number and waited.

'Hong Kong is eight hours ahead of us. It'll be night there,' Briony said hopelessly, helplessly.

'It's a news agency, isn't it? They never shut up shop,' Donna replied fiercely. She made the connection and thrust the receiver at Briony, 'There, now go for it. Track him down and make him tell you himself what's going on.'

Wavering between hope and despair, Briony took the receiver. 'Can I speak to Paul Deverill, please?'

'He's off duty.' The voice was male and sounded busy. 'Can I help?'

'No. . .' Briony almost put the phone down, but, because Donna was right and she really needed to know, she hung on to it. 'Did he leave another number where Briony Spenser could contact him?' She forgot for the moment she was Hammond now, but Paul wouldn't know that.

'He didn't leave a number for anybody,' the voice came back laconically. 'Do you want to leave a message?'

Briony shook her head, realised how stupid that was and managed to say, 'No.' All she could do after that was stare at the receiver.

Donna took it from her and said, 'When will Deverill be back on duty?'

'Nine o'clock tomorrow.'

'Thank you.' Donna slammed down the receiver and looked at Briony. 'Did you hear that?'

'Yes. I'll phone him tomorrow.' In a funny way she was glad she still had some shreds of hope to cling to. It would help to get her through the night.

It didn't help a lot, though. She tossed and turned, remembering and reinterpreting every word Paul had ever said to her. He'd never actually mentioned marriage, just that they would get together again in June and go to New York together. . .and he'd only committed himself that far after she'd slept with him.

In the darkness of her room, in a bed too narrow for her restlessness, it seemed to Briony that those were the words of a man already plotting his way out of a situation that had gone as far as he wanted it to. She could almost see Sheena in the background, waiting, smiling her knowing smile.

But then all Briony's instincts contradicted her thoughts. Her instincts whispered that Paul truly loved her, just as she loved him. She was on a mental and emotional see-saw all night long, and it was exhausting. She arose the next morning with only one thought—to find out the truth.

She phoned Paul before she went on duty. It was late afternoon in Hong Kong and this time she went through the agency switchboard. She asked for Paul and was put straight through.

'Deverill.' His voice came over the line as strong and powerful as the man himself.

A surge of joy she couldn't contain almost choked Briony. 'Paul,' she breathed huskily. 'Oh, Paul, it's Briony!'

There was a silence so deep she could hear the beating of her heart. Why didn't he say something? Panic-stricken, she said urgently, 'Paul, we have to talk.'

'Do we?' His voice was clipped, cold, impersonal.

She couldn't believe it. Desperately, she said, 'You know we do!'

He hung up on her.

The discordant buzz of the dead line rang in her ear, her head, her entire body. She hated it, but she still held on to the phone. She knew that when she put it down, when the quiet came, she would have said goodbye to Paul forever.

She couldn't do it, so she hung on to the phone as though it were a lifeline. Her lifeline. Finally one of the chambermaids came along carelessly jangling coins in her hand. She looked at Briony and the buzzing receiver and said, 'If you're finished. . .'

'Of course.' Briony was surprised how normal her voice sounded. She hung up and walked away.

It was a strange sort of world she walked into. A world of surviving minute by minute, hour by hour, day by day. She was totally out of touch with reality, but reality was there with her all the time.

She found herself avoiding Donna. Her friend's compassionate eyes mirrored a sympathy she couldn't accept, making her wish she'd never breathed a word about Paul. She wanted to hug her shame and her sorrow to herself, a personal burden she had no right to share with anybody else. No matter what happened, she couldn't alter her nature—and if she had to suffer, she preferred to suffer alone.

Everybody else thought she was grieving for Matthew. That wasn't entirely a lie, because she was. Her memories of him would always be precious, even if he had never had the power to shatter her the way Paul had done.

Life went on, though. She went quietly and efficiently through the mechanics of day-to-day living, revealing no sign of the turmoil raging within. She was being slowly torn apart, and sooner or later the crunch had to come. She knew it and ignored it.

She'd found a secret way to survive. Every night she escaped into a happier world where she was still with Paul, and the future still glowed. It was pure fantasy, and she knew that too, but it gave her the strength to get through the days.

She had other things to think about during her waking hours, and she did in a vague sort of way. Her contract was coming to an end. She had another job to find, and a bedsitter if it didn't include live-in quarters. Donna, in the same position as herself, had got a job as head receptionist at a large south coast hotel. She tried to contain her delight about it until Briony said wearily, 'Oh, for heaven's sake, you don't have to be miserable just because I am! I was a fool, but I'm getting over it. Nobody stays a fool forever.'

'If you're sure you're getting over it. . .' Donna replied hesitantly, wanting to be reassured because she was happy herself, but still doubtful.

'Of course I am!' Briony sounded so convincing she almost believed herself.

Donna certainly did. 'And—and Matthew?' she asked.

'I've come to terms with that too. I've accepted that everybody did the best they possibly could do at the time, including me.' Briony's voice faltered just for a second as she added, 'It's just not a perfect world, is it?'

Donna touched her arm. Briony tried not to flinch. Funny how she could take just about everything but sympathy. 'Something good will happen for you,' her friend said, absolutely convinced. 'You're due for a lucky break if anybody is.'

Strangely, it came that very afternoon. Mr Mathers, the hotel manager, sent for her. Normally such a summons would have made Briony apprehensive, but she was beyond all that now. Perhaps because she knew that nothing or nobody could ever hurt her the way Paul had.

'Ah, Mrs Hammond,' Mr Mathers said as she walked into his office.

Mrs Hammond. . .everybody called her that now, but it still had the same touch of unreality as when Matthew had slid the ring on her finger. Two weeks had passed since that day, and she still felt as much of a fraud.

'I've recommended you for an assistant manager's vacancy at our main hotel in Mayfair,' he went on. 'It means you'll have to start again from scratch, doing a few weeks in each of the different departments, but it's a step up the ladder and the opportunities for real advancement are limitless.'

Briony knew it and was stunned. She could only falter, 'Th-thank you.'

'Thank yourself, my dear. I've never heard anything but good about you from our guests and staff here, and I've nothing but admiration for the way you've conducted yourself since your husband's sad demise.'

Sad demise—what quaint old-fashioned words! She wondered how Mr Mathers would react if he knew she'd felt she'd been dying herself these past days, but from an entirely different reason. She checked her wayward thoughts and thanked him again.

'Nonsense,' he replied. 'You've earned this opportunity. I wouldn't risk my own reputation by recommending anybody I had the slightest doubts about.'

So, still with that strange sense of unreality, Briony left the Kensington hotel for the Mayfair one. There were no live-in quarters for her this time, but with her salary increase she managed to find herself a reasonable bedsitter just south of the Thames in Southwark. She wasn't much bothered, anyway. A palace wouldn't have meant anything to her without Paul.

Mr Mathers had certainly been right about one thing. She was treated as though she had no experience at all and was put on a rota that shuffled her through all the various departments that made up a world-renowned hotel. She was started in the housekeeper's department, where her entire working day seemed obsessed with ensuring that such things as linen and china were up to standard.

She did it all very well, but automatically. She had something else on her mind now, something she didn't dare believe was true. All sorts of things could account for it, particularly the traumas of Matthew's death and Paul's defection, but. . .

It was during the first week in June that she dared to believe, and went to see a doctor. She didn't have to wait long for the results of the tests and she was in a daze when she got them. They changed her entire negative views on the future she'd so far refused to look into.

She was carrying Paul's child.

She'd lost her lover, but his child was growing within her. She was overjoyed. It was a crazy reaction when her career was just beginning to take off, but she was beyond rational thought. She had a reason for living again, a reason for admitting to herself even during the harsh light of day that her love for Paul hadn't diminished by one iota.

More than that, it gave her the courage to contact him again. She'd no thought of trapping him because she was carrying his child. Much as she yearned for him, she didn't want him that way. In fact, it never even crossed her mind. She was simply carried away by the wonder of the moment.

It enabled her to believe what she'd always secretly believed, that if they saw each other again, looked into each other's eyes, then love would once more overwhelm them the way it had during those golden days in Paris.

She didn't know what had happened to Paul since then, whether Sheena had got her painted hooks into him or what, but she didn't doubt something had happened, something she didn't know about.

The difference was that now she had the strength and conviction to fight back. Briony looked again at the photograph of Paul and herself. During these past weeks when she'd been lost in an emotional wilderness the photo had been touched and caressed so often it was more crumpled than ever. But it still told the same story, whatever the evidence to the contrary.

The story of two people in love. She thought of the other photograph, the one Paul had kept. That told the story even more vividly. Somehow she was certain he still had it. . .and not because a hunter liked to keep a trophy.

Briony, buoyed up in a fantasy she refused to believe was better kept until after dark, phoned Hong Kong. She'd no idea what she was going to say to Paul. She only knew she had to hear his voice.

Even if it only said 'Deverill' again in that impersonal way, it would be something, and she was desperate enough for just about anything.

But the Hong Kong office told her that Paul Deverill was already in London, a week ahead of schedule. His father had been ill and Paul had returned to take the workload off his shoulders.

Briony was sorry about his father but thrilled Paul was so close. She looked up the agency's London number, then closed the book with a decisive snap. She didn't need to phone. She would go to see him, right now while her courage was so high. It was her day off. She wouldn't have the chance for another week, and who knew what soul-destroying doubts and fears would crowd in on her by then?

She was rushed and dishevelled when she arrived in Fleet Street, propelled by an inner conviction that refused to consider anything but seeing Paul again. There was nothing special about the off-the-rack cotton frock she wore, but there'd been nothing special about her clothes in Paris either. Such things had never mattered between her and Paul.

She stood on the pavement opposite the agency's tall building, staring up at the windows and wondering which of them belonged to Paul's office. Impatience overcame her and she crossed the narrow road, dodging cars and reaching the far pavement slightly breathless. It wasn't the breathlessness of exertion, but excitement.

She was so sure everything would be all right. She just had to see Paul, Paul just had to see her, and the magic would begin again. . .

In that instant she saw him. He pushed open the

agency's impressive glass doors and came out. The little cry of joy in her throat almost choked her as she saw that Sheena was with him. Sheena. . . Briony couldn't believe it. She was wearing a patterned silk dress that was a touch too dressy for a bright summer's day, but she looked every bit as magnificent as she had at the party in Paris.

Briony, about to rush impetuously towards Paul, checked and stood still. Nothing in her night-time fantasies or daytime hopes had prepared her for this. She paled as Sheena's bright blue eyes swept over her, a swift dismissive glance from top to toe. Her lips curved into that hateful, knowing smile and she slipped a possessive silk-clad arm through Paul's.

It hurt so much, that self-possessed gesture of ownership, but Briony's hungry eyes moved to Paul. Her Paul. He was every bit as handsome as she remembered, but there were lines of tiredness about his eyes and mouth. She thought she understood them because his father had been ill, and she yearned to reach out and smooth them away.

Her hands were reaching for him of their own volition when he saw her. Her heart beat so crazily she thought it would burst, and her teeth caught her bottom lip and bit into it in an effort to control her surging emotions. She saw those beloved grey eyes blaze, or thought she did, and waited for him to cast Sheena aside and grab for her. She ached so much to be in his arms that she swayed towards him, incapable of restraint. Not that there was need for any. She'd always known it would be like this. . .once they saw each other again.

But the only thing that happened was that Paul's

eyes went dead. He looked at, through and beyond her with no sign of recognition at all. She might have been a total stranger—she who had lain in his arms and shared every emotion it was possible for a woman to share with a man.

This man who had taught her how to live was now teaching her how to die. And, like the good pupil she was, she felt as though she were dying, inch by inch, heartbeat by heartbeat.

Through a fog of disbelief she saw his cold eyes turn from her to Sheena. She watched him drop a kiss on that coiled fair hair, put his arm around those silken shoulders and lead her away.

Briony almost felt that kiss, almost tasted it. It should have been hers, but it was Sheena's. She felt betrayed and robbed and cheapened. Worse than that, she felt naked. Paul had deliberately stripped from her the last pitiful vestiges of defensive pride that had kept her going.

Somehow Briony found herself walking away. She didn't know where or why, only that she had this terrible need to walk away from herself, this woman Paul didn't want. She wanted to become an automaton again. It was too painful being a real human being.

She walked until she could walk no more. In her exhaustion she found she was still human enough to be consumed with a hatred for Paul Deverill that was every bit as annihilating as her love for him.

# CHAPTER ELEVEN

BRIONY wanted just two things out of life. She wanted her baby and she wanted her hatred of Paul Deverill to last. The baby was her future, the hatred masked her love. By concentrating on both she was able to get through the following days, even though she felt like a zombie, the living dead.

She finished her stint in the housekeeper's department and was shifted to the restaurant. She donned the black dress, white pinny and cap of a waitress and waited on tables. Two weeks 'out front', she was told, another two weeks in the kitchens and she would be moved onwards and upwards. It was all part of sustaining the hotel's proud boast that its managers could do any job in any department.

Briony drifted with the days, knowing she would never stay the course. Strangely, her slender figure was more willowy and waif-like than ever, but she was three and a half months pregnant and it was only a matter of time before she began to round out.

Slowly, through the mind-dulling fog of her apathy, it was beginning to dawn on her what she wanted to do. She'd never had any real roots, but her spirit had always belonged in the country. She began to yearn for green fields, wide skies and fresh air. A place where purple and yellow pansies grew, a treacherous inner voice whispered, just as they had in Paris when she'd told Paul all about the cottage and garden she'd always dreamed of.

Without much hope, she'd answered an advertisement for a cottage in Norfolk, her home county. The owner was going abroad and wanted a careful, caretaker resident for a year. It seemed the ideal place to have her baby.

She was trying very hard to think of the baby only as hers. Paul didn't want her, so how could he possibly want the baby? He was still too busy living his own life to the full to want to be responsible for anybody else's.

She could see now that he used charm and frankness to make a virtue of self-interest. Like a child, he reached for what he wanted regardless of who got hurt. Still like a child, he got it, and was loved. Everybody else had to grow up and be responsible. But not the Pauls of this world, never the Pauls. They carried on charming and playing and getting away with it like perpetual Peter Pans.

The only solace Briony got in those grim days following Paul's blatant rejection of her was the secret knowledge that Sheena wasn't half as smart as she believed she was. She still thought she could land Paul. Briony knew better. She still had the unshakeable conviction that for a little while Paul had loved her. It still hadn't been enough, so what chance did Sheena have?

It wasn't much to hang on to, but it gave Briony a certain bitter satisfaction. It wasn't as though she had anything else going for her at that time. Then, on a Tuesday two weeks after she'd last seen Paul, she had a reply from the owner of the cottage. He was coming down to London and would like to meet her. Her hopes surging, Briony phoned and made an appointment before she went on duty at midday.

Oh, if only she could get the cottage! Life wouldn't seem half so grim! She tried to dampen down her hopes, fearful of disappointment, but as she donned her uniform and made her way to the restaurant she was more optimistic than she'd been for a long time.

She picked up her tray, notebook and pencil and walked into the luxurious restaurant, always particularly busy at lunchtime when non-residents came in for meals. The hotel was a top spot for business entertaining.

Briony's mind was completely obsessed with the cottage. If she got it—if? She must!—she was wondering if she would be allowed to quit her job instantly on compassionate grounds. She was certain she would. Mentally she was already in Norfolk, weeding the garden, making things for her baby.

It was then that she saw Paul. He was sitting at a table that wasn't in her section and staring at her with cold dead eyes that pierced her to the bone. She iced with shock and then began to tremble. What little colour she had in her cheeks fled and she felt naked, just as she had on that awful day in Fleet Street.

This couldn't be happening, she thought. She was imagining things. But there he sat. Handsome, solid, real, his dispassionate eyes surveying her as though she were some unrecognisable form of microscopic life.

Her step faltered. She could feel herself falling

apart, breaking into uncoordinated pieces that wouldn't obey her will. It wasn't hatred that was doing this to her, it was love. She could feel it burning through her as wildly and uncontrollably as it had burned in Paris, as it would always burn as long as she lived.

Briony knew that in her helplessness her eyes were appealing to his. It wasn't an appeal that was answered. Dear heaven, he looked as though he hated her! Was she supposed to have vanished off the earth when he had finished with her? Was it her fault if he came across her unexpectedly, reminding him of a time he clearly wanted to forget?

She expected him to get up and leave, but he remained exactly where he was, glaring at her in that implacable way. It was only when the waitress responsible for his table approached him that he looked away.

It was like being released from a spell. Briony found she could walk again, although she was still in a trance-like state. She went numbly about her own work, glad she didn't have to pass anywhere near his table, trying to forget he was there.

It was like trying to forget to breathe.

Again and again her eyes were drawn to his. They were always on her, always cold. She began to think he'd come here just to look at her, but that was crazy. If Paul had something on his mind he would do something about it. He was much too positive to take a passive watcher's role.

Then what the hell was going on? Briony's brain seethed but produced no answers. For nearly two hours she endured his clinical gaze, and then when she sneaked yet another look at him his table was empty. She waited for relief to flood over her, but all she felt was loss.

Paul hating her was better than no Paul at all—but why on earth should he hate her? He'd shut her out of his life, not the other way around. He'd never contacted her the way he promised. He'd hung up on her on the telephone, cut her dead on that dreadful day in Fleet Street.

If he was having second thoughts now he was going about it in a funny way. No, it couldn't be that. Whatever Paul was, he wasn't bizarre.

Briony went off duty several hours later with her head still in a whirl. She had served lunches, afternoon teas and set tables for dinner without conscious recollection of any of it. She went straight to her room and stared at the crumpled photograph of herself and Paul that she'd never managed to tear up and throw away.

It had been too much of a talisman, too much of a link with Paul, for her ever to harm it. But now, it seemed, Paul was trying to harm her. *Why?* She couldn't begin to guess, and she found no answer to the puzzle in the handsome face smiling at her from the photograph.

For a while she tried to tell herself she was over-reacting to Paul's presence in the dining-room, but she knew she wasn't. She only had her instincts to go on—but that was all she'd ever had with Paul!—and they told her he hadn't come to the hotel by accident. He had a purpose, just as there was a purpose in everything he did.

If only she could think what that purpose was! She

couldn't, though, and the puzzle teased her all through the night and into the next day. She was distracted as she served breakfast, dropping cutlery, rattling the crockery on her tray, mixing up the orders like an amateur.

She stumbled her way through to her mid-morning off-duty hours and hurried to her room to change out of her uniform. She had an appointment with the owner of the Norfolk cottage at a hotel in a quiet backwater of Bloomsbury. She'd been surprised at the haste, but he'd explained that the tenant due to take over the cottage had let him down at the last moment and he was contracted to go abroad himself.

Somehow, Briony had visualised an older man, but Arthur M. Frobisher, as he'd signed himself in his letter, was in his early thirties. He didn't seem interested in discussing anything but his garden and was delighted when he discovered Briony was a fellow enthusiast. Half an hour later she walked away with the keys to the cottage and the right to take possession on Saturday.

She'd given him an advance cheque that had halved her savings and she had no idea how she was going to manage financially in the long term, but she shelved that problem for another day.

She was acting on impulse, an impulse every bit as crazy as her trip to Paris. Again she needed to get away from everything and everybody she knew, but this time as a means of escaping the unbearable tensions of the past weeks. She feared she would crack up completely if she stayed.

When she got back to the hotel she went straight to see the manager. He wasn't available, but his assistant, Miss Stimpson, made time for her. She was a tall, gracious woman in her forties, and Briony always thought she looked more like a guest than an employee.

She wasn't expecting much sympathy, but she was wrong, perhaps because her desperation to get away came so vividly through her request to leave as soon as possible that it couldn't be mistaken for some kind of trivial excuse. Miss Stimpson already knew she'd been married and widowed, and when she learned that Briony was pregnant her face softened.

'You can finish when you come off duty on Friday, if you're sure that's what you really want,' Miss Stimpson told her. 'In my opinion it's a very rash thing to do. If you remain with us your job will be protected and we'll take you on again after the baby is born.'

'Thank you, but I'll be looking for a different kind of work,' Briony replied, dazed to be released so quickly, 'something part-time so that I can spend as long as possible with my child.'

She left the office a few minutes later feeling a great deal better than when she'd walked in. Getting the cottage, being able to move in this weekend, had turned her whole life around. All her aims and ambitions had shrunk to just getting there. It was a bolt-hole she couldn't disappear into quickly enough.

She was breathless when she rushed into the restaurant with seconds to spare at noon—breathless and fearful. But there was no Paul Deverill looking at her with baleful eyes. The relief was tremendous, although not quite as tremendous as the searing sense of loss that struck her once again.

It wasn't exactly a shock to realise she was only truly alive when Paul was close, but she lived in hope of the baby becoming some kind of compensation. In a way it was, but the moment her eyes fixed on that empty table she knew that, much as she wanted the child, she still needed the man.

Paul wasn't there on Thursday either, although by this time she wasn't expecting him. Tuesday must have been a chance visit, after all, an exclusive place to lunch for a man who moved in exclusive circles. She remembered with painful clarity how he'd said he hated to lunch alone.

Perhaps he'd hoped to pick somebody up, just as he'd picked her up, and seeing her there must have cramped his style. It would explain why he'd stared at her so long and hatefully. And yet. . .and yet. . .she would have sworn Paul wasn't vindictive, that he was more the type to laugh and go on his way.

But what did she knew about the real Paul Deverill, anyway? Nothing, except that he could lift her up to the stars and then let her fall and fall and fall. . .

At least she had plenty to do during her lonely off-duty hours. She'd already pruned her personal belongings when she'd moved from the Kensington hotel into her bedsit. She pruned them again, managed to cram her entire life into two crates and had them collected for delivery in Norfolk on Saturday.

She'd retained only her uniforms, which she would have to hand in, and a few items of personal clothes.

She would be able to travel to the cottage as lightly as she'd travelled to Paris.

Oh, Paul, her heart cried. Why? You loved me, I know you did. Are you one of those people who can only love lightly and never for long? Was that why Sheena was so confident? Because she knew that when you marry it will be to somebody suitable. Which she is and I'm not.

And when, oh, when will the hurt stop?

There was a certain grim determination about Briony on Friday. All her life she'd had such few ties, and she was about to cut the last of them. She worked the breakfast and lunch shift and only had to get through the afternoon teas and then she was free—free to pack her final oddments for an early start to the cottage the next morning.

To her, the cottage represented a clean sheet, a chance to start again. Owing to her chaotic upbringing, she had already had so many new starts that she wondered how she could still hope that everything would turn out right in the end. Deep down she knew she had no such hopes at all. It was just that her present life had become insupportable. She had to do something—anything!

Midway through her shift she had the feeling she was being watched. Her mind leapt to Paul and she looked around swiftly, but saw only strangers sitting at the tables. She couldn't relax, though, and inexorably her eyes were drawn towards the doors.

There he was, as somehow she'd known he would be ever since the strange feeling had come upon her. He was just standing there watching her, perfectly at ease with that inborn assurance she envied so much. Her own nerves began to jump. She looked hastily away from him and continued clearing and resetting a table.

She sensed rather than saw him crossing the huge room. A shiver of anticipation that began at the base of her spine and spread upwards and outwards to all her tingling nerve-endings told her he was close. Just how close she didn't know until he sat down at the table she was tidying.

'This table isn't quite ready yet, sir,' she said, switching on to professional automatic reflex but still feeling a colossal fool. What a ridiculous thing to say to a man who had held her in his arms and loved her as she'd never been loved before or expected to be again. But how could she treat him as anything but a stranger? It was what he wanted, wasn't it?

Then what was he doing here?

Her mind was as jumpy as her body as he replied, 'I'm in no hurry. I can wait.'

'Paul. . .' she said beseechingly, the myth that she could ever treat him as a stranger exploding as she dared to look fleetingly at him.

'So you remember who I am. I'm flattered,' he replied.

Briony's mind reeled all over again. 'Paul, please!' she whispered, but she didn't really know what she was pleading for. She was too confused, too over-whelmed by his closeness.

'You look terrible, Mrs Hammond,' he went on with a coldness, a repressed anger, she couldn't understand. 'Can't your husband care for you better than this? Or is it the nights that have put those shadows under your eyes? I seem to remember myself how abandoned you can be at night.'

Briony's pale face flamed. But while indignation and embarrassment robbed her of what little composure she had, some deep recess of her mind registered that somehow Paul had discovered she was married. What he didn't know was that she'd just as suddenly been widowed. This knowledge might offer her some kind of defence against his onslaught, if only she could figure out what was motivating him.

Then, in a blinding flash, it came to her. Sheena had said it was being promised to another man that had made her irresistible to Paul. That was the goad that had made him stalk her until she'd succumbed. Once he'd destroyed her allegiance to Matthew and made her his own, presumably she was supposed to stay that way—forever Paul's, even though he no longer wanted her.

It must have been a colossal blow to his ego when he'd discovered eventually that she'd married Matthew. Since he did not know the circumstances, it was his ego that was smarting, demanding redress. That was why he was here. That was why he was hounding her. Because he thought she was Matthew's and she shouldn't be. She should still be pining for him.

In that moment of revelation Briony almost hated him. She certainly couldn't speak. What she felt was beyond words.

Paul made full use of her silence by saying insolently, 'Are you as abandoned with Matthew as you were with me? And does he know he has me to thank for the difference in you, little sleeping beauty that you were?'

'Stop it!' Briony said fiercely. 'Just stop it!'

Paul's dark eyebrows rose. 'Do I take that to mean you're already regretting your hasty marriage? I thought you might be, considering the way we were together, but that can always be fixed.'

'What do you mean?' she asked, her anger as hot as his was cold.

He took her hand, raised it to his lips and kissed her palm, his knowing eyes never leaving hers. Briony shuddered with delight, unable to help herself. Paul saw that shudder and smiled a hateful smile. Then with complete assurance he put a labelled key into her hand and closed her fingers around it.

'My key and my address,' he said. 'We know each other too well to be coy, my little love. You have certain appetites that will always bring you to me, and your husband might as well learn sooner as later that you're not the little angel you seem. When you're ready, I'll be waiting.'

*His little love.* What the hell did he know about love? Nothing! Briony went rigid with rage. How dared he treat her like some kind of whore? She sought for some way to annihilate him, and she found it. With no other thought on her mind but to hurt him as he'd hurt her, she said, 'I'm carrying Matthew's baby. You wouldn't want to be landed with that, would you? No, of course not! It just wouldn't fit that lover-boy image you have of yourself—so go rattle your key in somebody else's face! I'm just not interested.'

She slammed down her tray and rushed blindly from the restaurant, leaving Paul to extricate himself as best he could from a scene he'd never thought she would make.

# CHAPTER TWELVE

THE driver of the little bus set Briony down in the middle of nowhere and pointed to a lane overgrown with weeds and barely visible between overhanging hedges. It looked no more than a tractor track. 'Willow Cottage is just down there a pace,' he told her. 'I make a round trip twice a day and pass here at ten in the morning and three in the afternoon if you're wanting to get into town.'

Briony thanked him, waited until the bus had trundled off on its dusty way into deeper nowhere, then crossed the narrow road to the track. It had been hot enough on the bus, but at least some kind of breeze had refreshed her through the open windows.

As she trudged along the heat trapped between the overgrown hedges smote her oppressively. She had to watch where she was putting her feet. The ruts the great wheels of a tractor had made in winter mud were now baked hard, and the riot of swift-growing weeds made it difficult to see holes until she tumbled into them.

She knew all about country distances, and that 'a pace' could seem like a mile to a townie, but even she began to get exasperated as each meandering bend in the track revealed nothing remotely like a cottage—or anything else, for that matter.

The strap of her holdall began to cut through the

thin cotton of her blouse—and her jeans, which had
seemed ideal for travelling, began to feel as clammy
and oppressive as the afternoon. The holdall was
getting heavier with every step, but she knew there
wasn't a pair of shorts among the amazing amount
of oddments she'd found to cram into it at the last
moment.

The journey from London had been tiresome
enough without this—changing trains twice, then a
coach ride and finally the little bus. Her exhaustion
was more than physical, though. Mentally Paul had
been with her for every weary mile as she relived
again and again that dreadful scene in the restaurant,
puzzling over every word he'd said as she sought for
some different interpretation of the way he'd tracked
her down and hounded her.

She'd come up with nothing, and so here she was,
still reliving it, still searching for a clue that wasn't
there. Only Paul was there, in her mind and in her
heart. She wished passionately she'd never seen him
again after Paris. Since she couldn't forget him, she
would rather remember the man he was than the
man he had become.

A wasp buzzed around her sweating face, and
Briony swatted it away without seeing it. Her vision
was filled with harsh grey eyes that had once been so
tender. . .her ears rang with a cruel voice that had
once teased her to laughter. . .her body yearned for
the touch that had once made her feel so safe, so
loved.

Once. Just like the fairy-tales that began 'Once
upon a time'. No, *not* like the fairy-tales, Briony
corrected herself, they had happy endings. She

checked her thoughts abruptly, afraid they were running away with her. She'd come too far, and been through too much, to crack up now. She wouldn't let it happen, not when she was so close to the cottage where she could shut the door on the world and, she hoped, begin to heal.

Her thoughts had carried her ever deeper into the countryside, and as she rounded yet another bend she saw it was the last one. There was the cottage, every bit as picturesque as she'd imagined it. She stepped out with renewed energy, and as she got closer she began to wonder if it wasn't a bit too picturesque. Honeysuckle and ivy were running wild over the windows, and the garden was just as much out of control.

Strange for a man like Mr Frobisher, who had spent all their time together talking about roses, lupins and hollyhocks. Briony had expected to find the garden immaculate, at least. But there were her two crates by the front door, so presumably the delivery van had been able to bump its way along the rutted track, although she could imagine what the driver had said under his breath.

With relief, Briony dumped her holdall on one of the crates and fished in her handbag for the keys. The door swung open and she waited a few moments before going in. Mr Frobisher had said he would be vacating the cottage yesterday, but the place smelled as though it had been shut up for much longer than that.

She got queasy so easily these days she was probably imagining the smell was worse than it actually was. She took a deep breath and walked in, meaning to open the windows before she looked around, but she stopped dead inside the sitting-room, her lips parting in dismay.

The place was filthy. Newspapers and magazines littered the floor and furniture. There were food-caked plates, dirty cups and overflowing ashtrays everywhere. She'd never seen such unbelievable squalor. She'd paid good money for this, money she could scarcely afford, and it took her a while to actually believe what she was seeing.

Briony felt tears prick her eyes, but she fought them back. She'd learned the hard way long ago that it wasn't the slightest use feeling sorry for herself. It was better to get angry, and stay angry. No wonder Frobisher had talked so much about his garden, damn him! He could hardly talk about this pigsty. It was small wonder his prospective tenant had pulled out at the last minute. So would she have done if she'd had time to inspect the cottage first.

Grimly Briony began to open windows, stalking from room to room and finding each in an equally unspeakable state. Nausea made her feel ill, but there was nowhere she cared to sit down. She went out into the garden, slumped on a crate and buried her face in her hands.

When she felt better she walked around the garden with the dual purpose of calming herself down and allowing the foetid air in the cottage to clear. Then she went inside and began to clean. Mercifully there was electricity and the water boiler worked. There was also a vacuum cleaner and all the cleaning aids she could wish for. Why the hell did Frobisher have all these things if he never used them? Had his wife walked out on him or something, and he'd just let the place go?

By late that evening Briony had the kitchen and bathroom usable and the sitting-room vacuumed and cleared of clutter. She would sleep on the sofa tonight. The finer cleaning and the other rooms could wait. She was dead beat and starving. Fortunately she had a few basic provisions in one of her crates.

She'd found an old bike in the garden shed. She would use that tomorrow to get to a village the bus had passed a couple of miles before she'd got off. It wasn't much of a village, but she'd seen a shop and she didn't want to waste time going all the way to town until the cottage was fit to live in.

It took her three more days of hard work before she was satisfied, but she'd had her bonuses. All the modern equipment in the now-gleaming kitchen worked, including the washing-machine. She'd flung just about everything movable into that, and the fine weather had held, drying everything quickly.

And all the time she scrubbed and polished she told herself work was the best therapy. Chantal and Paul had been right about that, as she'd discovered weeks ago. Not that work deadened the mind, it just kept it too busy to scream, and sometimes she did feel like screaming, because Paul always seemed to be with her.

She constantly remembered things he said, but always with bitter irony. When she was at her most desperate she would hear him say, 'I deal in hard facts. The dreams I leave to others.'

'Shrewd you,' she would reply, as though he were actually with her.

And then he would say, 'It's no good sitting around waiting for things to happen.'

'Give me the chance,' she would retort, lifting yet another mat to take out on to the line to brush. The vacuum was game, but it couldn't cope with weeks of ground-in dirt. She wanted an immaculate home for herself and her baby.

Her baby. . .little Paul or Paula. She tried hard to consider other names, but they had no relevance, and she always came back to those two. Paul would be flattered if he knew. The fact that she had to give his name to his child would be a nice sop to his wounded ego.

Damn the man! Why did she have to love him so much? Why wouldn't he get out of her head and her heart and leave her alone?

On Wednesday Briony decided the cottage was fit enough to receive flowers and she went into the garden to pick roses and white daisy-like chrysanthemums. There were enough vases in the cottage to tell her a woman had once lived here who had loved flowers as much as she did.

After that she decided she'd reached the stage where she could pick and choose what she wanted to do, or just do nothing at all. Being Briony, she set about the garden. By mid-afternoon she had the lawns scythed and mown and the flower-beds on either side of the garden path leading to the front door weeded.

She loved gardening so much it never seemed like work to her, and she felt no more than pleasantly weary. She also felt a kind of content, or as much content as she was capable of with Paul haunting her so persistently. But enough was enough. It was time to bathe and rest.

She wallowed in the sudsy water until she began to feel very sleepy. As she towelled herself she studied her stomach. Yes, there was a slight rounding now, surely? It wasn't just her imagination any more, was it? Smiling to herself, Briony dressed in fresh shorts and a little top that left her midriff bare. She was beginning to get a tan, and she was glad of it. She'd hated the way Paul had told her she looked terrible on their last catastrophic encounter. It might have been true, but he didn't have to say it, did he?

Briony sighed. Paul again. Everything she did, thought, said or dreamed came back to him. She was beginning to wonder whether she really wanted to be free of him, or whether she was welcoming him into her mind because that was the only way she could possess him.

What a sick thought! And yet. . .

She was walking to the sofa to rest when her thoughts were interrupted by the sound of a car. She stopped and listened. Nobody ever came this way, or if they did, they could only be coming to the cottage. She went to the open door and looked out. Yes, there was a car bumping its way over the ruts to stop at the garden gate.

Probably he was lost, she thought, and went down to the gate as he got out of the car. He was a small, middle-aged man wearing a suit that was too hot for such a scorching day. His eyes flicked over her, taking in the lustrous hair tumbling loosely to her

shoulder, her mini-shorts and top, and her bare feet.
'Who are you?' he asked offensively.

Briony's dark eyebrows rose. 'I was about to ask
you the same question.'

'I'm Quentin Baxter, solicitor to the owners of
this cottage. Where's Arthur? I don't know what
fast one he's pulling now by getting you here, but it
won't work. The eviction order is still being enforced
this afternoon. The bailiffs will be here any minute.'

Briony blinked at him. The man must have a
touch of the sun! 'You must have the wrong cottage.
I've just rented this one from a Mr Arthur Frobisher.
I paid him an advance of a thousand pounds
and——'

'What did this Mr Frobisher look like?' the solicitor broke in abruptly.

'Early thirties, brown hair, rather crooked teeth
but a very pleasant man—or so I thought until I
discovered what a state the cottage was in. I've been
since Saturday cleaning it up.'

'You've been conned, young lady. The man
you've just described was squatting here. The real
tenants have been in temporary accommodation for
three months while I took the necessary legal steps
to evict him. Naturally they're anxious to move in as
soon as possible, so you'll just have to get out.'

Briony stared at him in disbelief. 'But I have
nowhere to go, and I can't afford to lose all that
money!'

'You should have checked his credentials before
you parted with a penny,' Mr Baxter told her
unsympathetically. 'You've been very foolish. The
man you call Frobisher is really Derek Arthur. The

best you can do is make a statement to the police, but I don't hold out much hope of your ever seeing Arthur or your money. Meanwhile, I really must insist you move out, or I'll be forced to take legal proceedings against you too.'

Briony's stunned mind reeled as she absorbed the full horror of her predicament. She had no home, no job, and she'd lost half of her savings. She thought of all the hard work of the past days and shook her head in dumb disbelief. She heard another, more powerful car coming up the track. The bailiffs, she thought, feeling more alone and defenceless than she'd ever felt in her life.

It seemed there was a limit, though, to how much shock she could take. She saw a Range Rover draw up behind Mr Baxter's car, but it was swaying. So, too, was the big and powerful man who got out. Paul, she thought, and shook her head to try to clear her vision. Of course it wasn't Paul. It couldn't be. . . But she was thinking in slow motion now and the swaying world began to spin.

She reeled against the garden gate and everything went mercifully black.

Briony came to very slowly. She wasn't sure she wanted to. There was no pain in oblivion. She didn't want to open her eyes. She just wanted to be nobody, then nothing awful would ever happen to her again. Wishful thinking, she thought vaguely, but meanwhile it was so nice just to lie here and not have to do anything.

Where was she lying? Her brows drew together as she puzzled that one out. Somewhere comfortable.

There seemed to be a blanket over her, which was silly, because she'd been so hot. She could distinctly remember the heat that had overcome her before she'd pitched forward into darkness. What a silly thing to do! She'd never fainted in her life before.

There was something deliciously cold on her forehead, though. She sighed with pleasure. She'd just lie still a little longer, keeping the hateful world at bay, snuggling deeper into this so cosy cocoon. She couldn't remember when last she'd been so comfortable. All she needed was Paul with her and she would be in paradise again. She'd been there before with him. She knew what it was like. . .

*Paul*! Her eyes flew open as a hazy memory of a big and powerful man getting out of a Range Rover came back to her.

She found herself staring straight at him. No memory at all, no imagined companion, but Paul himself. Solid and real and so dearly loved, even though he didn't love her.

*Didn't love her.* Briony tried to struggle up. 'You shouldn't be here!' she accused. 'This is my safe place. Oh, n-no, it isn't,' she contradicted herself as full memory came back to her, and her voice wobbled. 'They're g-going to throw me out!'

Paul's big hands clasped her shoulders and pushed her gently back among the piled-up cushions. She shuddered at his touch, remembering other times, other moods. He misinterpreted and removed his hands swiftly. 'Nobody's going to throw you out of anywhere. You're quite safe. All you have to do is lie still until the doctor gets here and everything will be fine.'

Briony ran a distracted hand through her hair. She didn't understand any of this. 'What doctor? I don't need a doctor. I'm all right.'

'Is that why you fainted in my arms? I got that idiot of a solicitor to give me the number of the local doctor and called him on my car phone. He's on his way now. Just relax. There isn't a thing you have to worry about any more.'

He sounded so calm and confident Briony almost believed him. Then she shook her head as she realised she couldn't. She bit her lip, remembered he had once said he always wanted to kiss her when she did that, and her eyes filled with tears.

'Don't cry, Briony,' he said. 'I can just about stand you fainting in my arms, but I definitely can't stand you crying.' He took her hand in his old familiar way to kiss, recollected himself and put it down again.

She felt the old familiar tug at her heart, followed by a surge of disappointment, and unconsciously sniffed her tears away. It was a very childish thing to do, but she was feeling very childish. Not safe at all, no matter what he said, and extremely insecure. 'You don't understand. The bailiffs——'

'Baxter has sent them back. They had no power to touch you, anyway. The eviction order isn't in your name. I've sent Baxter off with a flea in his ear too, for frightening the life out of you.'

'I was so scared,' she confessed. 'I've nowhere else to go, and I've lost so much money.'

'No hassle,' Paul said soothingly. 'We'll figure all that out later.'

*We*? Briony thought. There is no '*we*'!

Indignant, she lay quietly while he changed the cold compress on her forehead. Its icy freshness chased the last cobwebs from her brain and she started thinking rationally again. Paul was assuming all too much. Just because she'd been temporarily helpless he seemed to think he could take over.

He was sitting beside her on the sofa, his arm resting on its back as he leaned over her. It was all too intimate. She was melting, just as she always did when he was close. She thought of him carrying her into the cottage, of herself lying in his arms, and nearly swooned away again.

She must stop being so stupid!

When the compress was in place she said, 'Thank you,' with the polite formality she would have used towards a stranger. To reinforce the message, she pulled the blanket under her chin and moved as far away from him as possible.

Paul understood. His eyes went bleak, but he stood up and moved to an armchair. Briony was both relieved and cross. Silence fell between them. They were certainly behaving like strangers now, and awkward ones. Still she wasn't satisfied. There were so many things unsaid between them, so many things she wanted to accuse him of, but she was terrified of getting personal.

She couldn't endure the silence, though, so she sought for a relatively safe subject. 'I gather Baxter told you how I've been cheated?'

'He was horrified when you fainted, and I wasn't too happy either,' Paul said in masterly understatement. 'Naturally I wanted to know what had been going on. Don't blame yourself for being taken in by

Arthur, though. You were in a vulnerable condition and that made you an easy target. I can't tell you how sorry I am for my part in it.' He paused, then continued quietly, 'I had no idea when we last met that Matthew had died. All I knew was that you married him. I was so devastated I wanted to get back at you any way I could.'

They both turned their heads towards the door at the sound of an approaching car. Briony wanted to concentrate on that, but her bitterness welled up and she couldn't stop herself snapping. 'You mean your ego was devastated! That's why you're following me, why you can't let me go.'

'My ego?' Paul repeated blankly. 'What the hell are you talking about?'

'You know very well, and there's no need to shout!'

'I don't, but I'm sorry I shouted. The last thing I want is to upset you again.'

'Again?' Briony closed her eyes in disbelief. 'When have you ever stopped?'

A knock sounded on the door, and she wished it hadn't. Her mood had changed and she didn't think she would ever feel really better until she screamed and raged at Paul, released all this tension inside her. Now she'd started, she didn't want to stop.

Paul seemed relieved, though. He went to the door and stepped outside to talk with the doctor before he let him in. Briony could hear the murmur of their voices, and she seethed. How dared they discuss her as though she were some kind of mindless idiot? Anyone could be allowed one swoon in a lifetime, surely!

The doctor when he came in, though, was so gentle and kind that all her hostility faded away. She found herself talking to him as she hadn't talked to anyone since she'd poured out her heart to Donna. Paul had had the consideration to stay outside in the garden. When she finally finished, though, she felt so much better that an examination seemed pointless. She was examined, anyway, and then spoken to quietly and reassuringly.

There was nothing basically wrong with her. She just had to rest and not overdo things. 'I don't have the temperament of an invalid,' she said frankly. 'I like to be busy.'

'There's nothing wrong with being busy,' the doctor told her, 'just so long as you rest when you're tired—and I mean tired, not exhausted.'

Briony understood. She thanked him and said goodbye, and watched him as he went out. Again that quiet murmur of voices drifted back to her, and again she felt resentful. The doctor seemed to think Paul was some kind of friend. Dear lord, he was so much more than that, and so much less. . .

She was off the sofa and in the kitchen boiling water for tea when Paul came back into the cottage. 'You never learn, do you?' he said. 'I can do that.'

'I'm perfectly capable——' But that was as far as she got. Paul picked her up, carried her back to the sitting-room and put her back on the sofa.

'Don't move,' he ordered.

She did, but only slightly. She sat up and watched him resentfully as he went back into the kitchen. She was *not* going to think how blissful it had felt to be in his arms again or how good it was to have her burdens lifted from her shoulders. This was the man who had loved her and dumped her. *Nothing* was going to make her forget that.

When Paul came back he put the tray on a side-table, handed her a cup of tea and took his to the armchair that was a reasonably safe distance away. 'You're suffering from stress, shock and exhaustion and you've refused sedatives,' he said quietly.

'I don't need them,' she replied defiantly.

'You need something. You have a baby to worry about as well as yourself.'

'Do you think I don't know that?' she flung at him.

'Drink your tea,' was all he said.

Thwarted, Briony did drink it and put the cup down. Paul's refusal to quarrel with her had its effect. 'I'm all right now,' she said quietly. 'There's nothing to keep you here. You can go.'

'I want to take you with me,' he replied, equally quietly.

His words hung on the air between them. Briony stared at him in disbelief, then said with a calmness that surprised herself, 'You know, Paul, I'm beginning to think you have a very bizarre sense of humour.'

'I never felt less like laughing in my life,' he replied, equally calmly. 'You've been through hell, and I want to do what I can to help. You have no husband, no home, very little money and a child on the way. I can give you all the things you need if you marry me, and I promise to bring Matthew's child up as my own.'

Briony was stunned. Then fury brought her to her

feet on one fluid, graceful movement. 'Good grief,' she breathed, 'the lengths your ego will drive you to! Is this the only way you can get back at a dead man?'

Paul came to his feet as well. 'I wish you'd stop raving about my ego. I love you! Why the blazes do you think I've been following you around like a sick calf? Because I can't stay away from you, that's why!'

'Love!' she repeated scornfully. 'What do you know about it? If you had the slightest notion of what it means you would have phoned me on that Monday when you promised you would.'

'I did.'

'*What*?' Dear heaven, Briony thought, on top of everything else he was lying now. 'You don't expect me to believe that, do you? You left no message.'

'Are you surprised?' Paul took her by the shoulders, roughly at first, and then the pressure eased as he recollected himself. 'I was told that Miss Spenser had married by special licence and was Mrs Hammond now. Did you expect me to leave a message after that? All I could think of was the way we'd been just two days before. I'd have felt a prize idiot if I'd even left my name. You left my arms, went straight into his and married him!'

Briony's legs weakened with shock. She would have fallen if his arms hadn't strengthened around her and held her up. Her eyes clung to his, searching for a truth she didn't dare believe. 'But when I phoned you, you hung up on me.'

'I loved you, and you were somebody else's wife. You'd promised me you'd never marry for anything but love, so what was I supposed to think? Well, I can tell you what I thought, Briony. I thought I was your last fling before you married and settled down in suburbia to the safe little life you'd always craved. I might have hung up on you, but what I really wanted to do was wring your neck. I loved you, for pity's sake!'

Briony stood frozen, wanting to believe, unable to believe. 'I came looking for you. . .to the agency. You were with Sheena, and you kissed her.'

'I was still flamingly angry with you, and I'm not the type to wear my heart on my sleeve. I was only taking her for lunch because she'd completed an assignment for us, but I used her to make you think I didn't give a damn about you.'

Paul shuddered, then continued, 'But you haunted me, Briony, every minute of every hour of every day. You drove me to that hotel in Kensington to find you again and I discovered you'd moved to Mayfair. I went there, hoping I could finally accept that you were somebody else's wife and let you go, but I couldn't. The more I looked at you, the more convinced I was you were mine.'

'Paul,' Briony breathed wonderingly, 'is this really true?'

'Take my word for it,' he replied unsteadily, 'I've lived it. I tried to stay away from you, but I couldn't. I tried to armour myself by thinking all the worst things about you I possibly could, and that's why I gave you my keys last Friday. What I really wanted was any part of you I could get, for as long as I could get it.'

'I didn't know,' she whispered, thinking of all the

agony she'd suffered herself and the defences that she too had thrown up. 'I thought it was your ego that was making you hound me, because I'd loved you and—and——' She choked, words failing her.

'My ego?' Paul gave a shaken laugh. 'You don't think I have any left, do you? It was only after you flung my keys back at me that I learned what you'd really been through. Some kind of manager came to smooth over the scene. He told me how you'd been widowed just after your marriage and were under a lot of stress. You can imagine how I felt!'

Briony, still afraid to believe the message the wild beating of her heart was telling her, said, 'That was last Friday, Paul. This is Wednesday.'

'Yes, but I went back to the restaurant every day. You were never there. I thought you were off duty, but today I learned that you'd left. I went to see the personnel manager to find out where you were, but she wouldn't tell me. There was a letter on her desk, though, addressed to you. I read the address and here I am.'

That letter, she thought vaguely, would be her final pay cheque and national insurance papers. Such a tenuous link, but it had brought Paul to her. She felt the misery and trauma of the past weeks draining from her, leaving her so weak she couldn't speak.

'Briony?' Paul's hand came up to ruffle her hair in that old loving way, weakening her even further. 'I know it was arrogant of me to think I could drive Matthew out of your heart, but I loved you from the first moment I saw you, and I still do. I know you felt a kind of love for me, and if you just let me look after you now I'll do everything I can to make it come back. I'm not asking for anything more for the moment. . .just the chance to look after you, and your baby.'

Briony was suddenly strong where she had been so weak. There was just an inch between their bodies, and she destroyed it by pressing against him and hanging on to him for all she was worth. There were so many things to say, but how to say them? Somehow the words tumbled out. At least, the most important ones.

'Oh, Paul, it's our baby. I only said it was Matthew's to hurt you. It was awful of me, but I was hurting so much myself.'

'*Ours*?' Paul prised her away from him and turned her face up to his.

She nodded, speechless again for a moment. Then, because she had to, because she needed to chase away all the last doubts between them, she continued, 'Matthew was critically ill when I got back to London. He wanted so much to marry me, and his surgeon told me the only chance Matthew had was his will to live, and I must do all I could to strengthen it. I had to marry him. I couldn't contact you to explain, not then. I could never have truly been his wife, but I'd have broken that to him later when he was well again. I thought that if you loved me as I loved you, you'd have understood and waited until I could get a divorce. Only. . .' Her voice quivered.

'He died. My poor darling, what you've been through!'

'What we've both been through,' said Briony, her

eyes moistening with tears. 'But it's over now, isn't it?'

'It's over,' Paul agreed, his lips coming down to claim hers, so gently and tenderly that she marvelled how many facets there were of love. Then he raised his head, his grey eyes mirroring the love she felt for him, the love nothing had ever been able to break. 'I thought I had nothing,' he said huskily, 'and now I have a wife and a baby.'

Briony caught her breath. 'I'm not your wife yet, my darling.'

'You've been my wife since I first saw you that rainy day in Paris,' Paul said positively. 'It's just that I've been longer claiming you than I expected.'

His searching, possessive lips came down on hers again. Briony felt well and truly claimed at last.

It was a lovely feeling.

HARLEQUIN
*Romance*

**HARLEQUIN ROMANCE
LOVES BABIES!**
And next month's title in

# THE BRIDAL COLLECTION

brings you *two* babies—and, of course, a wedding.

**BOTH OF THEM
by Rebecca Winters**

**THE BRIDE** objected.
**THE GROOM** insisted.
**THE WEDDING** was for the children's sake!

Available this month in
THE BRIDAL COLLECTION

**LOVE YOUR ENEMY
by Ellen James**

Harlequin Romance #3202
Available wherever
Harlequin Books are sold.

WED-3

OVER THE YEARS, TELEVISION HAS BROUGHT
THE LIVES AND LOVES OF MANY CHARACTERS INTO
YOUR HOMES. NOW HARLEQUIN INTRODUCES YOU
TO THE TOWN AND PEOPLE OF

One small town—twelve terrific love stories.

GREAT READING...GREAT SAVINGS...
AND A FABULOUS FREE GIFT!

Each book set in Tyler is a self-contained love story; together, the
twelve novels stitch the fabric of the community.

By collecting proofs-of-purchase found in each Tyler book, you can
receive a fabulous gift, ABSOLUTELY FREE! And use our special
Tyler coupons to save on your next TYLER book purchase.

Join us for the fifth TYLER book,
BLAZING STAR by Suzanne Ellison, available in July.

*Is there really a murder cover-up?*
*Will Brick and Karen overcome differences and find true love?*

# HARLEQUIN
## *Romance*®

## Coming Next Month

**#3205 FIREWORKS! Ruth Jean Dale**
Question: What happens when two blackmailing grandfathers coerce a dashing rodeo cowboy and his estranged Boston-society wife into spending time together in Hell's Bells, Texas? Answer: *Fireworks!*

**#3206 BREAKING THE ICE Kay Gregory**
When hunky Brett Jackson reenters Sarah's life after ten years, he brings a young son, two dogs and a ferret. His questionable reputation comes, too—which doesn't make him the kind of guy for whom an ice maiden should melt....

**#3207 MAN OF TRUTH Jessica Marchant**
Sent to Switzerland to promote a new vacation package, Sally has no idea she'll have to confront Kemp Whittaker. Film producer, TV presenter, nature lover and every woman's fantasy, he opposes Sally and everything she stands for. Can she withstand his assault?

**#3208 A KIND OF MAGIC Betty Neels**
Fergus Cameron's arrogance makes him the kind of man most women find annoying, and Rosie is no exception. Admittedly, he can be charming when it suits him—not that it matters to her. Fergus has already told her he's found the girl he's going to marry.

**#3209 FAR FROM OVER Valerie Parv**
Jessie knows that no matter how hard she tries, there's no way to stop Adrian Cole from coming back into her life. She knows she wants a second chance with him—but she's afraid of his reaction to her son, Sam.

**#3210 BOTH OF THEM Rebecca Winters**
Bringing home the wrong baby—it's got to be a one-in-a-billion chance. Yet Cassie Arnold's sister, Susan, believed it had happened to her. With Susan's tragic death, Cassie's obliged to continue her sister's investigation. And she discovers, to her shock, that Susan was right; her real nephew is living with divorced Phoenix banker Trace Ramsey, as his son. When Trace becomes aware of the truth, he insists on having *both* children. There's only one solution, he says—Cassie will have to marry him....
*Both of Them* is the third title in The Bridal Collection.

---

**AVAILABLE THIS MONTH:**

**#3199 A CINDERELLA AFFAIR**
Anne Beaumont

**#3200 WILD TEMPTATION**
Elizabeth Duke

**#3201 BRAZILIAN ENCHANTMENT**
Catherine George

**#3202 LOVE YOUR ENEMY**
Ellen James

**#3203 RUNAWAY FROM LOVE**
Jessica Steele

**#3204 NEW LEASE ON LOVE**
Shannon Waverly

## BIG SUMMER READ

## Summer Reading At Its Best

In July, Harlequin and Silhouette bring readers the Big Summer Read Program. Heat up your summer with these four exciting new novels by top Harlequin and Silhouette authors.

**SOMEWHERE IN TIME by Barbara Bretton**
**YESTERDAY COMES TOMORROW by Rebecca Flanders**
**A DAY IN APRIL by Mary Lynn Baxter**
**LOVE CHILD by Patricia Coughlin**

From time travel to fame and fortune, this program offers something for everyone.

Available at your favorite retail outlet.

BSR

## "GET AWAY FROM IT ALL" SWEEPSTAKES

# HERE'S HOW THE SWEEPSTAKES WORKS

### NO PURCHASE NECESSARY

To enter each drawing, complete the appropriate Official Entry Form or a 3" by 5" index card by hand-printing your name, address and phone number and the trip destination that the entry is being submitted for (i.e., Caneel Bay, Canyon Ranch or London and the English Countryside) and mailing it to: Get Away From It All Sweepstakes, P.O. Box 1397, Buffalo, New York 14269-1397.

No responsibility is assumed for lost, late or misdirected mail. Entries must be sent separately with first class postage affixed, and be received by: 4/15/92 for the Caneel Bay Vacation Drawing, 5/15/92 for the Canyon Ranch Vacation Drawing and 6/15/92 for the London and the English Countryside Vacation Drawing. Sweepstakes is open to residents of the U.S. (except Puerto Rico) and Canada, 21 years of age or older as of 5/31/92.

For complete rules send a self-addressed, stamped (WA residents need not affix return postage) envelope to: Get Away From It All Sweepstakes, P.O. Box 4892, Blair, NE 68009.

SWP-RLS

- - - - - - - - - - - - - - - - - - - - - - - - - - - - - - - - - - - - - - - - - - - -

## "GET AWAY FROM IT ALL" SWEEPSTAKES

# HERE'S HOW THE SWEEPSTAKES WORKS

### NO PURCHASE NECESSARY

To enter each drawing, complete the appropriate Official Entry Form or a 3" by 5" index card by hand-printing your name, address and phone number and the trip destination that the entry is being submitted for (i.e., Caneel Bay, Canyon Ranch or London and the English Countryside) and mailing it to: Get Away From It All Sweepstakes, P.O. Box 1397, Buffalo, New York 14269-1397.

No responsibility is assumed for lost, late or misdirected mail. Entries must be sent separately with first class postage affixed, and be received by: 4/15/92 for the Caneel Bay Vacation Drawing, 5/15/92 for the Canyon Ranch Vacation Drawing and 6/15/92 for the London and the English Countryside Vacation Drawing. Sweepstakes is open to residents of the U.S. (except Puerto Rico) and Canada, 21 years of age or older as of 5/31/92.

For complete rules send a self-addressed, stamped (WA residents need not affix return postage) envelope to: Get Away From It All Sweepstakes, P.O. Box 4892, Blair, NE 68009.

© 1992 HARLEQUIN ENTERPRISES LTD.

SWP-RLS

## "GET AWAY FROM IT ALL"

### Brand-new Subscribers-Only Sweepstakes

# OFFICIAL ENTRY FORM

This entry must be received by: May 15, 1992
This month's winner will be notified by: May 31, 1992
Trip must be taken between: June 30, 1992—June 30, 1993

**YES,** I want to win the Canyon Ranch vacation for two. I understand the prize includes round-trip airfare and the two additional prizes revealed in the BONUS PRIZES insert.

Name _____

Address _____

City _____

State/Prov. _____ Zip/Postal Code _____

Daytime phone number _____
(Area Code)

Return entries with invoice in envelope provided. Each book in this shipment has two entry coupons — and the more coupons you enter, the better your chances of winning!
© 1992 HARLEQUIN ENTERPRISES LTD. 2M-CPN

---

## "GET AWAY FROM IT ALL"

### Brand-new Subscribers-Only Sweepstakes

# OFFICIAL ENTRY FORM

This entry must be received by: May 15, 1992
This month's winner will be notified by: May 31, 1992
Trip must be taken between: June 30, 1992—June 30, 1993

**YES,** I want to win the Canyon Ranch vacation for two. I understand the prize includes round-trip airfare and the two additional prizes revealed in the BONUS PRIZES insert.

Name _____

Address _____

City _____

State/Prov. _____ Zip/Postal Code _____

Daytime phone number _____
(Area Code)

Return entries with invoice in envelope provided. Each book in this shipment has two entry coupons — and the more coupons you enter, the better your chances of winning!
© 1992 HARLEQUIN ENTERPRISES LTD. 2M-CPN